PIRATE SEALER

"*Get back!*" *Staton warned as Tubby began to inch forward.*

(*See page 66*)

PIRATE SEALER

by

ARTHUR CATHERALL

THE CHILDREN'S PRESS
LONDON AND GLASGOW

For CHRISTIAN AGERSKOW and the crew of the *Frobisher*, with whom I sailed the Northern waters.

Bolton, 1951

Printed in Great Britain

CONTENTS

CHAPTER ONE

LAST NIGHT ASHORE

THE quiet waters off Tromso were speckled with the green, red and white riding lights of a hundred vessels, making that normally quiet haven a miniature fairyland of colour. There were vessels of fifty tons, and vessels of three hundred and fifty tons. Though some of the smaller craft looked little more than fishing smacks, within a week they would be pushing their way through the mush ice, down north, looking for seals.

Inshore, on a shelving beach, a five hundred ton vessel was beached. Her decks were ablaze with light, and over the side a vividly blue-white light flashed and sparkled mysteriously. Up to their knees in the icy cold water two be-goggled men stood and patiently welded a patch on the vessel's bows.

Some ten hours earlier the trawler *Lady Hope* had been steaming down one of the fjords between Hammerfest and Tromso, after a successful fourteen days off the Murmansk coast. A sudden fog, combined with a strong inshore tide, had taken the *Lady Hope* too close to a razor edge of rock. From then until she was beached at high tide to the north of Tromso, only her powerful pumps had kept her afloat.

When the receding tide was low enough the engineer, Tubby Fenner, and his "second," Stan Farrager, had gone over the side with the portable welding kit, and worked with desperate speed to patch the damaged plates.

There was no question of the trawler limping across the North Sea unless she was efficiently patched, for it was late winter, with savage gales possible at any time.

At length Tubby Fenner pushed back his goggles. Stan Farrager flashed his torch over the "patch," examining it with the greatest care. On its seaworthiness depended a "clearance" from the Norwegian surveyor, who would come aboard when the tide served. He would say whether the ship could sail or not.

"I think she'll do," Tubby muttered. "Come on—I'm gasping for a cup of char and a bite."

Climbing aboard, the two engineers washed and changed. They had a meal, and then went below to listen to the pumps. The pumps were gasping a little now, pointing to the fact that the last of the sea water was being sucked out of the bilges.

Marshall Trayne, the trawler skipper, joined them, and nodded to show his satisfaction when the gasping pumps were finally shut down.

"Think she'll be all right, Fenner?" he asked.

Tubby Fenner, a giant of a man, with a strong Geordie accent, laughed.

"'Course she'll be all right," he said. "When I do a job, Mr. Trayne, it stays done; you can bet your last shirt button on that." He grinned at his "second," then followed the trawler skipper up on deck.

Up there the air was keen with the nip of a Norwegian winter. The stars twinkled from a clear sky, while the lazy reflections of red and green side lights were now beginning to break up into long ripples as the rising tide brought in a slight swell.

"Like to slip ashore for an hour?" Trayne asked, waving his pipe in the direction of Tromso. "Should be interesting. According to the pilot, the sealers are in for their last night before going out."

"Sealers?" Stan queried.

"Wait till you're married," Trayne chuckled, "and have to buy your wife a sealskin coat . . . you will remember these fellows, then. Must make a fortune out of the game . . . though they can have it for me. A shocking life, if all I hear about it is true. Anyway, if you'd like to stretch your legs—you can. According to the pilot it's a sort of gala night in Tromso. The sealers gather here to sign on, and make whoopee. It's the last chance they get for a month or two."

"What do you say, Tubby?" Stan asked.

"Join the Navy and see the world," Tubby chuckled. "Come on! Though I don't suppose there'll be much to see but whiskers, or anything to hear but *skoal*."

"*Skoal*. What do you mean?" Stan was puzzled.

"What an innocent," Tubby jeered. "*Skoal* is the Norwegian for 'Here's mud in your eye!' 'Good luck!' 'Bottoms up!' and so on. Boy, you're not eddicated. Come on—it's time we showed him a thing or two, Skipper!"

"Hm! Well, don't take him to the wrong places," Skipper Trayne warned. "I want two working engineers back aboard by midnight. The surveyor will be here at half twelve, and if everything is all right, I'm off with the tide."

"There's a fellow for you," Tubby mocked, turning to Stan. "He asks us to take a walk ashore—to see the Paris of the North, and then says we've got to be back within a couple of hours."

"Doesn't look much like Paris to me," Stan pointed out, as he went for his scarf and cap. And, indeed, seen from the beach, Tromso looked little more than a sleepy village. The lights were few and far from brilliant, even though the snow, which lay on the roofs and streets alike, tended to make the scene more romantic-looking.

Ten minutes later the burly Tubby was leading Stan into the streets of Tromso. The wind blew cold, and they pulled up their coat collars.

"Some Paris of the North!" Stan grunted. "Not a shop nor a cinema to be seen! I think old Trayne was pulling our legs when he sent us ashore. We——"

"What's that?" Tubby stopped, and cocked his head on one side like a dog hearing the sound of its master's footsteps.

Stan listened, and the frown vanished. Faint on the still, cold air, came the rollicking tune of a jig. The two Britishers hurried up the hill, and as they drew nearer the wooden building from which came the music, they realised that somebody really was making "whoopee."

A fiddle was screeching against a background of raucous voices, the thump of fists on tables, and even the shuffle of heavy-booted feet.

"Great dancers, these Norwegians," Tubby explained, as they hurried across the well-trodden snow, to where two great patches of yellow lamplight streamed out from uncurtained windows. "And when they get 'lit-up' I believe they're great scrappers, too. Anyway, if it looks too rowdy we won't stay."

Stan grinned. Tubby Fenner was one of those men who seemed built for trouble. The Geordie had the proportions of a young elephant and the habit of finding his way into one dockside row after another, yet he invariably came out unscathed.

Pushing open the swing doors Tubby stood and stared, while a blue fog of tobacco smoke rolled past him into the night. The air was heavy with the smell of beer and spirits, and it was difficult to see to the far end of the room, so thick was the smudge.

For the moment the fiddler was resting and the dancing had stopped. Men were crowded about the small tables, talking animatedly, while perspiring waiters dashed about with trays loaded with schooners of beer. There was a constant clamour for more drinks. Every man seemed in a hurry to drink as much beer as possible before putting to sea.

Tubby found two seats by the window, and ordered coffee. The sweating waiter lifted his eyebrows at the word "Coffee," nodded, and hurried away.

"Funny thing," Tubby mused, lighting a cigarette, "I'll bet there isn't a man in this room could afford a sealskin coat for his wife—yet before they come back here at the end of the sealing season, every man jack will have hauled hundreds of seal pelts across to his ship—aye, mebbe thousands of 'em."

Stan nodded. He was staring about him in wonder. A good proportion of the sealers looked oldish men, white-haired, but lean and wiry. There were plenty of beards, and every moustache visible was of the generous, old-fashioned type, reminding Stan of the pictures he had seen of Vikings.

"They reckon sealing is so tough it makes winter trawling seem like a kids' game," Tubby muttered, nudging Stan to draw his attention.

"Hm!" Stan was scarcely listening. Looking idly about the room he had thought for a moment he had seen a familiar face. Yet, when he looked again, he could recognise no one.

"What's the matter?" Tubby asked, as Stan half rose, to get a better view across the crowded room.

"I thought I saw a chap I used to be friendly with," Stan murmured, then sat down again as the waiter arrived with the coffees.

Across the room, however, the man whom Stan had thought he recognised was speaking exult-antly to a companion, while keeping his head lowered.

"Thorson, we're in luck. I knew something would turn up . . . and it has. I've just spotted the very man we need."

"A diesel engineer?" his companion asked, looking swiftly about. "Where is he, Jimmee? Did he see you?"

"I don't care whether he did or not," was Jimmy Staton's retort. "He's a diesel man, and if we can get him aboard the *Bear*, everything will be all right. Come on!"

"You think he'll come with us?" Thorson queried, rising to his feet as if to go across to Stan and Tubby.

"Here—you fool!" Staton snapped. "He mustn't see us, yet. Stan Farrager won't come with us of his own free will. More likely he'd tip off the police."

"Well, what's the——?" Thorson began, then turned to follow his companion to the back door. Once they were outside he asked:

"Now, Jimmee, explain . . ."

Jimmy Staton laughed cynically:

"He won't come of his own free will. If you want a first-class diesel man, you'll have to grab him."

Thorson frowned, and after a moment Staton made a suggestion:

"You get back to the *Bear*. Bring half a dozen of the boys, and I'll watch for Farrager coming out. Be as quick as you can. Farrager won't stay here for long . . . he isn't the boozing sort."

"I'll meet you at the corner of Amundsen Street and the alley that runs down to the coaling wharf," Thorson said.

"Right, but be quick."

Thorson ran off while Jimmy Staton went to the front of the building, and found a sheltered spot where he could watch, yet remain unseen.

Sipping their coffee by the window, Stan and Tubby stayed longer than the waiting Staton had imagined. The two Britishers were most interested in the men about them. They had the stamp of sea-rovers on faces and clothes. They drank and they talked, and it was obvious that most of them were meeting again for the first time since the end of the previous sealing season.

Stories were being told, reminiscences exchanged, while beer flowed like water. The word *skoal* seemed to be in the air all the time.

Then, without warning, there was a commotion

which stilled every tongue. In the farthest corner of the room two men were quarrelling. One man stood up, and was promptly hit over the head with a heavy glass beer schooner.

In a moment the men were divided into two camps, and for once even Tubby Fenner recognised the danger signals. He rose, grinned, and began to move towards the door.

"If we hadn't to be back to a time, Stan," he cried, halting by the door, "I'd have loved seeing the end of this little row. I'll bet there are broken noses and busted heads by the dozen."

"Out!" Stan ordered, and pushed Tubby against the swing door. "If we don't move now the *Lady Hope* is going to be without two very efficient, if underpaid, engineers. Come on!"

They pushed out into the night, while, in the room they had left, the row was developing fast and furious. Men were fighting; tables were being pushed over, and there was the crash of breaking glass.

"The trouble with England," Tubby chuckled, "is that there are too many policemen. You start a row, and in no time at all you're in the jug, cooling your heels till morning. Here—well, I'll bet the police keep as far from the pubs as possible —for a night like this, at any rate."

They swung off downhill, the lights of the anchored sealing vessels acting as a sure guide to the waterfront. Tubby was just getting into his stride in a story concerning a row he had been in at Trincomalee, during the Hitler war, when a voice from a dark alleyway halted them.

"Farrager! I say, is that Stan Farrager?"

"Who's that?" Stan halted, then gave a low cry as he recalled the voice, and connected it at once with the face he had seen in the tavern. "Is that Jimmy Staton?"

"Yes. Keep quiet. Come across here for a moment. I want to talk to you."

Stan hesitated, and Tubby gave him a gentle push.

"Go on, I'll wait."

Staton was standing in the gloom of the narrow alley, and he gripped Stan by the arm the moment they met. In an urgent whisper he said:

"Look, Stan, I'm in a hole. Will you help me? It won't take more than a few minutes. I'd do the same for you, any time, you know I would."

"What is it?" Stan asked, suddenly very uneasy. "I'm due aboard in a few minutes. We're sailing on the tide."

"Come on—I'll tell you while we're walking," Staton whispered. "You won't miss your boat. You're off the trawler, aren't you—the *Lady Hope*? I'll get you back in good time, but I don't want any one else to see me just now. Tell your pal you'll come on later."

Tubby, whose hearing must have been acute as a cat's, promptly strode across.

"Look, matey," he said briskly, "if you're in trouble, and you are a pal of Stan's—okay. You

can count on me as well as him. One thing—he's
not going away on his own. Now, what's your
trouble? We haven't a lot of time to spare."

"Well," Staton coughed, as if embarrassed, then
suddenly brought his right arm round in a wild
swing. In his hand he held a sock filled with wet
sand.

Stan ducked instinctively, but Tubby, just
behind him, never saw the sock until it was too
late. He took the full impact of it right in the
centre of his forehead, and sat down, dazed.

Staton went backwards to a full-blooded punch
in the nose as Stan hit out angrily. Then the
darkness seemed full of men. A brutal fist took
Stan on the side of the jaw, a punch in the ribs
sent him reeling. As he stumbled another man
caught him, and clapped a big hand over his
mouth, stifling the cry he was starting to make.

Tubby Fenner was half-way to his feet when
another blow from the sand-filled sock put him
down for the count.

"Get the ropes and gags, quick," Staton panted.
"We don't want to be caught like this."

"Nobody about," Thorson assured him, but the
men obeyed Staton's injunction to hurry, and
within a couple of minutes the two Britishers
were bound and gagged.

"Down the main street," Staton ordered. "No
use trying to hide them. If we see a policeman
he'll take them for drunks, there'll be plenty of
them in Tromso to-night."

Five minutes later the eight men, carrying Tubby and Stan, walked boldly past a policeman standing near the quay. He laughed quietly when informed the two men were drunken sealers, and volunteered the information that there would be plenty of sore heads aboard the sealing ships when morning came.

He waved them a cheery good night as the two prisoners were lowered into a small boat, prior to being rowed out to the *Bear*, Thorson's diesel-engined vessel, anchored a quarter of a mile from the shore.

CHAPTER TWO

SHANGHAIED!

WITH no undue haste the overcrowded boat was pushed off and rowed through the crowds of shipping. Finally the *Bear* was reached. She was a vessel of some eight hundred tons, and vastly different from the majority of the sealing craft. There was an indication of speed about her lines. Her funnel was little more than eight feet high, and was squat-built. A pipe ran up the rear of the funnel, to carry away the fumes from her diesels. The funnel was merely a dummy to give the vessel shape, and to house a small radio room.

Without fuss the two Britishers were carried aboard and placed in separate cabins. The lights were switched off and, still bound and gagged, Stan and Tubby were left to recover.

Stan fought with his wrist bonds until sheer exhaustion made him stop. His bonds had been tied by a seaman, and no ordinary prisoner could have got out of them.

Finally, sleep brought relief. When Stan woke it was to see the dim shape of a porthole, grey in the light of mid-morning. Tromso in late winter has a day which starts in mid-morning and ends in mid-afternoon. So that when a thin, watery

sun began to stream in through the porthole Stan
knew it must be at least eleven o'clock, if not later.

Thinking of the *Lady Hope*, he groaned, and
wondered what had happened. Marshall Trayne
would have sent someone ashore for them, that
was certain. What was almost as certain, would
be the fact that no one would be able to give any
information about them. Possibly the waiter at
the tavern would remember them, but he would
not know whether they had been in the brawl
which had started just as Stan and Tubby left.

He was still trying to imagine why he was there
when the cabin door was opened, and two men
entered. Stan recognised the second man immediately. It was Jimmy Staton.

"Sorry for the discomfort, Stan," Staton said,
and began untying the gag which had chafed
Stan's mouth. "We had to keep you quiet. Didn't
want you telling the world you were here."

"Fetch him a drink, Jimmee," the tall man
suggested, and going to the porthole he stared
out, remaining like that until Staton returned
with a glass of water and a pint mug of coffee.

Stan managed to get into a sitting position.
His mouth felt raw, and his throat was stiff. To
be gagged for so long was one of the most un-
pleasant experiences he had ever known.

Gratefully he sipped the water. It was cool and
sweet, and it made him realise just how thirsty
he had been. Rage and worry had helped him to
overlook that unpleasantness until now.

"We make good coffee aboard this ship," Staton murmured as he held the pint pot to the prisoner's lips. "It is one thing the old cook can do well. Cigarette?"

"No." Stan had finished the coffee, which had been good, but he shook his head at the offer of a cigarette.

Staton took a cigarette, lit it, then turned to the man at the porthole.

"Meet Captain Thorson, Stan. He'll be your new skipper for the next month to six weeks."

Thorson turned at that, a smile on his dark face.

"I hope we shall be good friends," he said, and knocked the ash gently off the cheroot he was smoking. "I think we shall, to our mutual benefit, eh Jimmee?"

"You bet!"

"When you've finished this joke," Stan said quietly, "I'll be glad of an explanation, and it had better be a good one. You know Shanghai-ing went out of fashion a long time ago. You're in for a lot of trouble very soon. My skipper will be turning Tromso inside out at this minute," then as his forced calm deserted him for a moment. "Have you both gone crazy? What sort of a mad stunt is this?"

"It isn't a stunt," Staton said. "Just listen calmly, Stan. I think I know exactly how you feel, but maybe you'll feel a bit different when I tell you that for a month or six weeks aboard our ship you're going to get five hundred quid. Just think of that—five hundred quid."

"And you'll get five years in jail," was the tart reply. "What's the idea, you lunatics?"

"Tell him," Thorson said coldly, and turned again to the porthole. He was watching the sealing fleet in process of weighing anchor. Long streamers of black smoke drifted over the water from the coal-burning vessels, blue diesel fumes from the smaller craft. Small boats bobbed about, as men who had been too drunk to get back the night before were now hastily rejoining their ships. Seabirds flew out, crying plaintively, and the blue sky seemed to suggest that it was not late winter at all, but mid-spring.

Then Staton began the explanation Stan was waiting for so eagerly.

"We're a diesel ship, and until yesterday morning we had one tip-top diesel engineer, and two greasers who can stop and start the engines, and that is about all. Our engineer had an accident, and is now in hospital. That left us with no engineer."

"And we must have a good engineer," Captain Thorson put in crisply.

"You see the position," Staton went on. "We were just about at our wits' end for a good diesel man when I saw you in the pub. I couldn't believe my own eyes for a moment. It seemed too good to be true."

"I didn't notice any eagerness to renew old

acquaintance," Stan said bitterly, and Staton grinned.

"No, I'm sorry about that," he chuckled. "Sight of you—just what the doctor ordered, so to speak, must have made me forget my manners for the moment. Anyway, we needed an engineer very badly. We didn't think you'd come of your own accord, so we just grabbed you. Hope your head isn't aching too badly."

"I still think you are crazy," Stan growled, "because there isn't a man breathing can *make* me look after diesels, and I tell you flat I'm not going to look after them aboard this ship. It's as much as my ticket's worth . . . it would mean I had agreed to desert the *Lady Hope*. Now, Jimmy, stop playing the fool. Cut me loose, and I'll get over to the *Lady Hope*. I don't know what will happen to you, and at this stage, I just don't care."

Captain Thorson threw his half-smoked cheroot through the open porthole, then turned towards the cabin door.

"I'll get under way, Jimmee," he said quietly. "Persuade this obstinate Britisher that he is coming with us. Further," and now there was an edge to Thorson's voice, "he needn't be too confident that we can't make him look after the diesels. We can, and will."

With that he went, closing the door quietly.

Stan felt a chill of something like real fear steal through him. It was all crazy, of course, yet

Thorson had sounded as if he meant what he said.

As if reading Stan's thoughts, Staton said quietly:

"He can be a good friend, Stan, and a bad enemy. Take my tip, come as our engineer. The job is for a month and you'll get a cool five hundred pounds for your part in the game."

"Game!" Stan snapped. "It stinks to me. It's crooked. It must be or you wouldn't use these darn fool methods. Come on, man, you're too decent to be mixed up in anything shady. Set me free, and I'll do what I can for you."

"For old times' sake, eh?" Jimmy Staton chuckled, but there was bitterness in that chuckle, bitterness and sarcasm. "No, Stan, I know I was with you in the old Scout troop, and all that sort of thing; but times have changed, and I've changed. I've had a raw deal, and now I'm on a good thing. There's no turning back for Jimmy Staton." He ground the butt of his cigarette beneath his boot, then said sincerely:

"Listen, Stan, throw your hand in with us, and you'll be rich in less than a year. That's gospel. Rich!"

Stan checked the sneer which came automatically to his tongue and asked:

"What's the racket? It must be a racket, or you couldn't talk like that and mean it. I know you well enough, Jimmy. You're not lying."

"Of course I'm not," Staton said, then turned

and began to pace the cabin. Finally he stopped opposite the bunk head.

"I'm going to give you the dope, Stan. It'll make you gasp, but once you see how simple it is, you'll understand why I say we can all be rich in no time at all. In a week, or less, this ship is going to become a Russian gunboat."

He paused, as if to see the effect of his words, and smiled grimly at the look of amazement on Stan's face.

"A Russian gunboat!"

"Exactly," Jimmy grinned. "And that Russian gunboat is going to extract a fortune from the seas around the White Sea just as easy as I'm lighting this cigarette. As easy as that," he repeated.

Just then, faint enough, but heard in the cabin, came the distant jangling of bells. Stan recognised them at once. They were engine-room telegraph bells, and he knew what they signified. Someone on the bridge had moved the telegraph lever over to: "Stand by engines."

Another, fainter jingle indicated that the signal had been answered. Then followed more bells. "Half-speed ahead," and almost immediately the cabin began to vibrate gently. The screws of the *Bear* were turning, churning up the icy water.

"Yes, we're on the move," Staton said, going over to the porthole and looking out. "Half the sealing fleet are on their way, and we're going with them. You can say ' Good-bye ' to Tromso,

Stan, and to the trawler. You're coming with us, now, whether you like it or not."

"I'm sorry for you," was all Stan could say, for there was a new fear gnawing at him. Up to this moment he had not really believed that he could be taken away against his will, even though his hands were still tied behind his back. He had clung to the thought that, at the very last moment, when he showed no signs of agreement, Staton and Thorson would release him.

Staton drove home that fear when he turned from the porthole:

"By the way, I forgot to tell you. That's your pal at the controls. He's agreed to take over the diesels." He nodded at Stan's sign of disbelief, "Oh, yes, it's true enough. He knows which side his bread is buttered on. Take my advice, Stan. Just think it over. You can't go back, no matter what you decide. Better come in with us. Thorson can be a good boss—but he can also be tough."

With that he turned and left the cabin.

For the remainder of that day Stan saw no one except a man who turned out to be the cook, and a small, dark-faced guard who stood just inside the cabin door, an automatic held in full view, as a warning that any resistance would be met with force.

The cook brought a belated breakfast, but took the coffee away when he saw that Stan's wrists and hands were so benumbed that they were quite useless for the time being.

Regaining the use of his hands was agony, but the cook came back, minus coffee pot, and began to massage the swollen wrists. His ministrations were effective and surprisingly gentle.

Stan tried to get him to talk, but his questions were ignored. Then, when Stan could once more use his fingers, the cook went out and returned with the coffee pot, from which steam was rising.

"Cold coffee ain't no use to nobody," he muttered. "Get that into you. You'll never get better coffee nor that, nowhere."

He left the cabin, but returned half an hour later, bringing a bowl of warm water, towel and soap. He maintained the same grim silence while his prisoner washed.

"I feel sorry for you," Stan told him as he gently laved his sore wrists in the soapy water. "When the Law gets its hands on Thorson, I'm afraid you'll all suffer. Every one of you."

The cook tugged at the shabby chef's cap he wore, looked at the guard by the door, and moved away. He stood quietly wiping his hands on a sweat rag, giving Stan a chance to take a good look at him.

He was a man in the middle fifties, though he might quite easily have been younger or older, for though his face was lined, when he moved he had a brisk enough walk, and carried himself erect.

Stan wondered if he might possibly be won

over. He was obviously proud of his coffee-making. That suggested he took a real pride in his job. Somehow that did not fit in with a scallywag, and Stan had decided that all who were aboard the *Bear* must be rogues of the worst kind.

The guard was with the cook at lunch-time, but did not come when tea was served. Stan decided that they were apparently too far from land for him to benefit by a rush out on deck.

A rising wind, and an equally rising sea, was making the ship roll uncomfortably, and when the cook came in with the tea he brought with him a flurry of snow. The door slammed shut, and if Stan had not steadied him the cook might have fallen.

"Thanks, mister. There. Sorry I can't give you better grub. I'm obeyin' orders." Then, as Stan sat down, the cook leaned over, wiped the table top with his apron and said: "We've just passed Hammerfest. Ever been there?"

Stan shook his head. If the cook was in the mood to talk he would give him every opportunity.

"Not much of a place," the cook went on. Then as the ship heaved up her bows to allow a great roller to pass underneath, he muttered, "It's thickenin' up outside for a bad night. The Cap'n is reckonin' on being round North Cape to-morrow morning. But if it keeps on like this, I doubts we'll do it."

Stan cut a slice of bread from the loaf, and as

if unable to think of anything further to say the cook turned towards the door. He paused there and asked:

"Ever met Cap'n Thorson before, mister?"

"No, and I can't say I like him now that I have."

"Wish I'd never met him," the cook muttered dolefully, and moving nearer the table, he went on confidentially: "If you'll take my advice, mister, you'll do what he asks, when he sends for you. He's goin' to have you and your mate in the big cabin. At least, they've set places for five of you, an' I had orders to bring your tea now, 'stead of later."

"He'll get no change out of me," Stan assured him, and the cook wagged his head sadly.

"He's a bad man to cross, mister. Take my tip on that. An' if you get a chance . . . tell that pal of yours what I say. It don't get you nowhere, crossing Cap'n Thorson. I know. He's a hell-cat."

"Where is Tubby?"

"Tubby?" the cook queried. "Who's he?"

"The other chap—he was brought aboard with me."

"Oh, your mate," the cook grinned ruefully. "Where is he, you asks. He's locked up, an' in irons, he is."

"I thought he was in charge of the engines."

"Lumme—him!" For the first time a look of genuine amusement drove the doleful lines from the cook's face. "Don't make me laugh, mister.

Why, when I took his breakfast there were a real
dust-up. Didn't wait for to get the use of his
hands. Oh, no. He ups and lights into the
guard, just as if the chap didn't have a gun or
anything. Fair paralysed me he did. I didn't
know what to do."

"And what happened?" Stan could imagine
Tubby leaping out just as the cook had said.

"Thorson stopped him," the cook's smile
vanished as if some spirit had drawn a veil over
it. "He's a swine, he is. Come rushin' in—an'
I'd the job of putting five stitches in your mate's
head after that. He's too handy with that gun
butt—too handy by half."

"Was Tubby badly hurt?"

"He ate his dinner all right," the cook assured
him. "Anyway, as I said before, you just listen
careful-like when you meets Cap'n Thorson, an'
don't argue with him. It'll save a lot o' trouble.
I'm warnin' you, mister, an' I knows."

Twenty minutes later Stan was escorted by two
armed men to the big stateroom, where Captain
Thorson awaited him.

CHAPTER THREE

THORSON'S CUNNING

STAN was amazed at the luxury of the *Bear's* stateroom. The ship had obviously belonged to some very wealthy man. The panelling was magnificent, the carpets opulent, while the table, at which sat Thorson and Staton, was the work of some great craftsman. Stan wondered how all this had passed into the hands of crooks. Then Thorson waved a hand to a chair.

"Sit down, Farrager," he said and his tone was friendly. "What will you drink? Whisky, brandy, gin and lime? We haven't a big selection, but what we have is good stuff."

"I don't drink, thank you," Stan said, and sat down.

Then Tubby Fenner was brought in. The Geordie's head was bandaged, and his wrists were in irons. He was scowling, but at sight of Stan he smiled, and winked.

"Well, well, Stan, congratulations! They tell me you've taken on the job of chief engineer. Promotion at last, eh?"

"Promotion my foot," Stan assured him. "I'm not touching this business with a barge pole."

"Good!" Tubby sounded relieved, then turned as Thorson spoke to him.

"Sit down, Mr. Fenner. Can I offer you a drink?"

"You can *offer* me a drink," Fenner told him, "but you won't unless you want the stuff spitting in your eye. If you want to make me happy, take off these handcuffs. I'll then enjoy punching your face out of shape."

"We'll talk business," Thorson refused to be ruffled, and turning to one of the men who had escorted Tubby into the room, he said: "Meet my first mate, Mr. Ivan Igorsky. One time mate aboard a Russian sealer. What he doesn't know about the Russian methods of sealing isn't worth knowing. What is more important, he knows the Murmansk coast and the mouth of the White Sea like you know the back of your hand."

Igorksy looked first at Stan, then at Tubby. He did not hold out his hand, merely nodded, a grim nod which held no friendliness.

Stan eyed the man over, and knew he would be a nasty person to be up against in a rough and tumble. He looked as if he had been hewn from a great chunk of granite. His shoulders gave the impression of terrific strength, while his hands were like spades.

Thorson interrupted Stan's thoughts, and there was a hint of irony in his voice as he said:

"Now that we are introduced, and *friends*, I'll

explain exactly what lies ahead, and thus avoid any mistakes or unpleasantness."

Igorsky and Staton nodded, Stan and Tubby merely looked straight before them.

"Very soon we shall put into a small bay off the Murmansk coast. We are well in front of the sealing fleet, and while they catch up, and pass us, my crew will change the appearance of the *Bear*. She will assume the look of a Russian gunboat."

He drew deep on his cheroot, then, when no one spoke, he went on:

"By the time the sealing fleet has been hunting for a day or so, we shall come on the scene. We shall be flying the Russian flag and will begin arresting sealing ships—all in the name of Mr. Joseph Stalin, of course. We shall confiscate all sealskins, and I am hoping we will soon be much wealthier than we are at the moment."

He knocked the ash from his cheroot, and looked expectantly at Stan and Tubby. When neither Britisher spoke Thorson's eyebrows lifted, and after another quick puff at his cheroot, he went on:

"Your job, my friends, will be to keep the diesel engine at concert pitch. I must have engines which can be depended upon, for a real Russian war vessel patrols the area, and if we encounter her, well, I would naturally want to show a clean pair of heels. For that reason, Mr. Farrager, I'm making you chief engineer."

Stan looked up, startled. He stared at Thorson for a moment, then looked at Tubby, before saying:

"I'm flattered, but apart from the fact that I am not as qualified as my friend, I refuse even to look at your diesels. That's my last word."

"I expected that," Thorson said, and smiled. It was not a pleasant smile; rather the smile of a cat which has a helpless mouse at its feet. "Just the same, I am promoting you chief engineer, and your fat friend will be hostage for your good behaviour."

"Hostage?" Stan was puzzled.

"According to my dictionary," Thorson said patiently, "the word 'hostage' means: 'A person given in pledge.' In other words, Mr. Farrager, the safety of Mr. Fenner depends on whether you do exactly as you are told."

"Aw, take no notice of him," Tubby sneered, "he's been reading a book, or something."

"I have," Thorson admitted, "and I got this idea from a story book. It struck me as being very clever, and also most effective. That is why I am adopting it. I intend to put you ashore, Mr. Fenner, at a point on the Murmansk coast miles from anywhere—and, of course, it is winter. Not a nice time to be alone on the coast of Murmansk. However, if Mr. Farrager agrees to work for me, I shall leave you well supplied with food, and other necessities. Later, when our work is completed, I shall pick you up, and every one will be happy." He smiled, and leaned back in the big armchair.

Silence, save for the faint hum of the diesels, the whine of the wind, muted by the closed doors of the stateroom, and the occasional splash of water on deck. Finally, as it seemed there was to be no reaction from either Tubby or Stan, Thorson scowled, jerked erect, and snapped:

"All right. Take them back."

"Keep your chin up, Stan," Tubby urged, as he rose from his chair, his hands still secured by metal cuffs behind him. "I'll see this gang in the Juvenile Courts before a week's past. They haven't got past playin' Red Indians yet."

Igorsky gave Tubby a push.

"I wouldn't do that too often, my lad," the Geordie warned, "you'll ha' me losin' my temper."

Stan was hustled out of the stateroom, and gasped at the bite of the wind. In the short time they had been indoors it seemed to have doubled its velocity, and was screaming past in breathtaking fashion.

Back in his cabin he was glad to undress and climb into his bunk. As he lay in the darkness, with the ship rolling and occasionally burying her bows in the great combers, he wondered if Thorson really would put Tubby Fenner ashore.

Stan had only a slight knowledge of the Murmansk coast. He just knew it was both bleak and inhospitable. In winter, a time of long and bitter gales, a man without adequate shelter, heat and plenty of food, would soon perish there.

Rack his brain though he would, he could not think of any way out of the dilemma. He was a prisoner, and Tubby's bandaged head was evidence enough of what happened if resistance was offered.

Sleep put a temporary end to his worryings, and he awoke to find Ben, the cook, laying the small table. The breakfast was a vastly different affair from the previous day. Now there was coffee, porridge with tinned cream, sausages and tomatoes; then marmalade and toast to finish.

"Bit of a change in the menu," Stan suggested sarcastically.

"You gets the same food as the Cap'n and the others, now," Ben replied, and shot a queer glance from beneath his shaggy eyebrows as he asked: "Are you a-goin' in with 'em?"

Stan shook his head, and the conversation languished, apart from Ben volunteering the information that they were going in to the coast, and that the storm was just about blown out.

After he had shaved, with a razor borrowed from the cook, Stan was called out. The *Bear* was at anchor, and all movement had ceased. It was so calm as to make it hard to imagine that a few hours previously the ship had been tossing and rolling in a blinding storm. When he went on deck, in company with two guards, he could see the reason for it. The *Bear* was anchored in a perfect little harbour, entered by means of a narrow fjord. The shore was just visible in the grey light of morning. There seemed to be a narrow strip of beach, with snow-covered cliffs jutting skywards. A grim place indeed.

An hour's exercise on deck, then Stan was taken to his cabin again, while the crew went on with their work of transforming the vessel from a graceful-looking yacht to a dour, business-like gunboat.

A Bofors quick-firing gun was mounted for'ard, as well as several dummy guns. The bridge and funnel were cunningly altered. Paint was splashed about, and when the transformation was completed, the *Bear* would look like one of the smaller type Russian gunboats.

On the third day came the summons Stan had dreaded. He was called for'ard. Tubby Fenner was standing by a little heap of boxes and rolls of material. With him was Thorson, Ivan Igorsky, and several of the crew. Of Jimmy Staton there was no sign.

"Now, Mr. Farrager," Thorson was polite, but making no ostentatious attempt at friendliness, "make your choice. We are putting your friend ashore. He can go with food, or without. If he goes with food, clothing, tent and stove he may be bored but at least he will be well fed and warm. I don't need to tell you what will happen if he goes ashore empty-handed." He tapped ash from his cheroot, and waited.

Stan looked at Tubby and knew there could be

only one answer. Tough though the Geordie was, he would never survive without food and shelter.

"Look after the diesels," Thorson suggested, "and there will be nothing to worry about. We'll pick up Fenner when we return."

"He'll ditch you, first chance he gets," Tubby warned.

Stan sighed. He was between the devil and the deep sea, yet he could not let Tubby be marooned without food and shelter. He nodded agreement.

"You give me your word of honour, as an Englishman?" Thorson pursued the point relentlessly.

"Yes, I do," Stan snapped, and, turning to Tubby, he said apologetically: "Can't let you go ashore with nothing, Tubby."

Tubby nodded grimly.

"Okay, Stan. It's a case of any port in a storm. Anyway, don't worry," turning to Thorson he said: "Well, I'll get moving. The air should be a bit sweeter ashore. I never did like the company of skunks." With that he cocked a leg nimbly over the rail, and slid down to the waiting boat.

One by one the boxes and packages were lowered to him. Then three of the crew followed, two to take the oars, one to sit in the stern, an automatic pistol ready. They were taking no chances with Tubby.

When the boat was bobbing on the quiet water Thorson turned to Stan: "Now, Mr. Farrager— the diesels. I know they need tuning. I want them at their best. If we should meet the real Russian patrol ship, we'll have to trust to our engines. I am armed, but I prefer to run rather than fight. Make a good job of everything." Then, as Stan turned towards the door leading to the engine-room, Thorson added, "If we were caught, I'm afraid no one could possibly rescue our Mr. Fenner."

The sarcastic inflection he gave the words made Stan feel like turning back and punching the man. Thorson's lip curled in a smile, and there was no doubt he was gloating over his victory.

It was pleasantly warm in the engine-room. Two men loafed in one corner. They put out their cigarettes and stared at Stan suspiciously.

Stan soon discovered their knowledge of diesel engines was confined to the controls. They could stop, start, reverse and little more.

For the rest of the day Stan checked and tuned. The diesels were a very fine piece of engineering work, British made, and not very old, but sadly in need of tuning.

He forgot some of his worries as he worked, for he was an engineer with a pride in his craft. It grieved him to see any piece of machinery which was not running like velvet. By the time he had given everything a first overhaul he estimated he could give the *Bear* a speed of seventeen or eighteen knots. A further tuning would increase that.

Checking the fuel tanks he was amazed to find

there was sufficient oil for a journey of several thousand miles. Whoever was behind this amazing venture had planned wisely, and had spared no expense to ensure its success.

When he finally left the engine-room, and went for a breather on deck, the short winter day had ended.

Wiping his hands on a lump of cotton waste, he was turning to go to his cabin, when he noticed a spot of yellow light ashore.

"Tubby," he whispered, and wondered how his Geordie friend was faring. A wind was whining through the funnel stays; a thin, cold, penetrating wind. How Tubby would fare if one of the late winter gales sprang up, Stan shuddered to think.

"I must do something," he decided, and went to his cabin to think. He had refused to dine with Thorson and Staton, so the cook had been instructed to serve Stan's meals in his cabin.

When old Ben brought the evening meal, he shook his head and jerked a thumb towards the porthole which faced the shore.

"How'd you reckon he'll go on, Mr. Farrager?" he asked, his voice a mere croak. "Wouldn't like it myself. Makes me shiver to think about it."

Stan could have kicked the man for his gloomy words, and the moment he had finished his meal he got ready for bed. Sleep was better than brooding helplessly over Tubby's plight.

Before getting into his bunk he looked through the porthole. The spot of yellow was still there and Stan visualised the burly Geordie crouched by his oil stove, trying to keep warm. It would be bitterly cold, for a bone-chilling wind was keening eerily out of the North.

"I'm not staying here," Stan muttered, turning to the door. "I'll take my chance with him, and——" he stopped as he realised the door was locked. Thorson was taking no chances of his new engineer deserting. Stan was still very much a prisoner.

The porthole was too small for escape, and more dejected than ever, he crawled into his bunk. The wind was moaning now. Soon it would be blowing a gale—and Tubby had only a makeshift tent.

Stan racked his brain for some way out of the mess until sheer weariness overtook him and he slept.

When he awoke some time later "gooseflesh" was crawling up his cheeks and neck. His hand went out to the light switch, but stayed there without depressing it while he strained his ears for further sounds.

Save for the slap of water against the hull, and the moan of the wind, the ship seemed to be absolutely quiet.

Stan was just beginning to think he must have been dreaming when he did hear a sound. The key in the door lock was being turned . . . turned very slowly, and very quietly. Yet, whoever was turning the key could not prevent the tumblers dropping when they passed balance point. In that strained quiet they were like bold clicks to the listening Britisher.

Very quietly he slid out of his bunk, and shivered as his feet touched the linoleum. His open porthole had reduced the temperature considerably, and the floor covering felt like ice.

Stan quietly pulled on his trousers. He sensed that the man who had unlocked the door was listening. There had been no sound now for more than a minute.

Then there was a movement of air. The door had opened, causing a draught from open port-hole to open door. The door closed, and Stan switched on the light. Momentarily dazzled, he blinked and gasped.

Facing him was a naked man. From head to foot he was shimmering green, like some mythical sea-god straight from the bed of the ocean. His torso rippled with muscles. He looked like some piece of Greek statuary suddenly come to life.

Stan opened his mouth to shout, and the strange being leapt at him.

CHAPTER FOUR

MUSH-ICE GHOST

"QUIET! Quiet, Stan!"

Two powerful hands gripped Stan by the throat, choking off his cry of alarm. "It's me—Tubby."

Stan, keyed-up to throw off this frightful figure, relaxed, and stood quivering. Then the slippery hands came away from his throat.

"Tubby?"

"'Course, who'd you think it would be?" Tubby Fenner asked. "I've been aboard half an hour, poking about, looking for your cabin. Cor! You didn't think I was going to stop ashore, did you? Why, man, it's perishin' in that tent—just plain perishin'."

His Geordie accent was sweetest music to Stan's ears, and he grinned.

"For the love of Mike, sit down. You scared the wits out of me. What's all the green stuff? It makes you look terrible. Here, I'll put the light out, in case anybody comes."

"Give me a towel," Tubby pleaded. "I'm fair shiverin'. And this green stuff—lor, I thought you'd have recognised that, man, it's lubricating oil. They gave me three cans of the stuff for my

45

stove. That'd drive any man to swim for his life. The fumes were terrible. Ah, thanks," as Stan gave him a bedsheet in lieu of towel. "Now, fetch my togs. I left them under the for'ard lifeboat, port side. I wrapped them in an oilskin sheet. I covered myself with this perishin' oil to keep out the cold, but I'm chilled to the bone, just the same."

Stan put out the light, went on deck, retrieved Tubby's clothing and got back again without being seen.

Tubby had wiped off the oil and was dancing about to restore the circulation to his chilled body. He dressed, then draped himself in one of the blankets from Stan's bunk. With the light switched off, they sat while Tubby smoked a cigarette, and controlled the chattering of his teeth.

"Well, I feel a thundering sight better now you are back," Stan told his friend, "but what can we do? If they find you aboard there'll be the——"

"Don't tell me," Tubby chuckled, "let me guess. Anyway, it can't be worse than being marooned across there. Man, it's just hell on shore. No place for Tubby Fenner. I'm not going back."

Stan shook his head in the darkness. Hiding was easier said than done, as Tubby knew well enough.

"If you was in complete charge of the engine-room," Tubby finally whispered, "we might have done something."

"You can stay here. Nobody else uses this cabin," Stan said quietly. "The only chap who comes in is the old cook, Ben somebody-or-other. He doesn't look the kind who'd do much cleaning up, and——"

"Too risky," Tubby insisted, at which Stan shook his head.

"It's the ideal place," he pointed out. "No one would dream of any one trying to hide here."

"I mean it's too risky for you," Tubby grumbled. "If they caught me, Thorson would vent his spite on you. He's that kind of fellow."

"We'll jump those fences when we come to 'em," Stan said firmly. "Look, I'm going to divide the bedding. You can have the bunk. I'll sleep on the floor. We'll be warm enough. The cabin is steam heated."

"What about food?"

"I eat in here," Stan explained. "I'll develop a terrific appetite and we'll divide all that is brought along. We'll just have to be careful when old Ben comes in. But I think you could hide under the bunk—we'll drape a blanket over the edge. We'll get away with it, Tubby."

"We might," Tubby agreed. "I'm lucky; but I'm not daft enough to think my luck will hold through a full voyage. We've——"

"Let's get some sleep," Stan urged. "We'll discuss all that later on."

Considering the upsets of the evening, Stan dropped off to sleep very quickly, and slept well, but morning brought a threat of discovery which neither he nor Tubby had thought of.

Tubby Fenner had an alarm clock mind. He was up betimes, and wakened Stan. When breakfast arrived, Tubby was lying under the bunk, hidden by the trailing end of a blanket, while Stan was staring out through the porthole.

There was a fiddling at the door. The key was turned several times, while the old man cursed to himself. Finally Stan grabbed the door handle and pulled the door open.

" What's wrong, Ben?"

To his amazement the cook walked across to the table, laid his tray down, gave the cabin a swift, all-enveloping stare, and snapped:

"Who have you had in here?"

"What?" Stan's pretended surprise was good, though it was not all pretence, for the old cook's remark had shaken him.

"You've had a visitor," was the prompt retort. "I locked this cabin door last night. It weren't locked now. I left the key in the lock."

"Well, you can bet your boots *I* didn't reach the key under the door," Stan chuckled, trying to make light of the matter. "You probably forgot to turn the key. In any case, I haven't escaped, so what're you worrying about?"

"Cap'n Thorson made me responsible for you, so I need to worry," was the growled reply. "Anyway, look at this . . . then tell me you haven't had a visitor."

He turned to the door, and pointed accusingly at the floorboards in the alleyway.

Stan looked down, and his heart dropped to his boots. Faintly visible in the electric light, were two footprints. Tubby Fenner had been dripping oil when he came aboard, and while he stood in the little alleyway, trying the lock, oil had dripped down his legs, so that two big footprints were well and truly outlined in oil for all to see.

"Ye can't deny that, can you?" Ben asked sourly, and then almost apologetically added: "I don't want to get nobody into trouble wi' Thorson; but I'll have to report it. I'd get into trouble myself if I didn't."

In the second or so which followed this declaration Stan Farrager's brain worked quicker than it had ever worked before. A search would mean the end of Tubby.

For a moment Stan thought of attacking old Ben, but dropped the idea immediately. Short of killing him, the cook could not be silenced permanently. Then, like a flash, he had an inspiration, a heaven-sent idea.

"Do you think it's *the ghost*?" he asked, and lowered his voice.

Ben stared suspiciously at Stan, one corner of his mouth lifted in a half sneer.

"Ghost?" he demanded. "What ghost?"

"You mean you haven't heard of the—the—the mush-ice ghost?" Stan was playing for time and trying to concoct some kind of convincing story.

"You've sailed in sealing ships before, haven't you?"

"'Course I have; but I've heard tell of no mush-ice ghost."

"Hm! No, you wouldn't," Stan said quietly. "That's the funny part of it. I'm a trawler man, and I know the story. I suppose sealers daren't talk about it."

"Daren't talk!" Old Ben was definitely interested now. "What do you mean? If there is a—a mush-ice ghost they'd talk about it. Are you pullin' my leg?"

"Don't be a fool," Stan pretended to be annoyed. "I don't care tuppence whether you believe me or not. As far as I can see, the sealers who got to know about the mush-ice ghost didn't talk because . . . well, they didn't live to talk."

Stan was beginning to get his story into shape.

"Here, what are you drivin' at?" Old Ben belonged to a race of seamen fast dying out, men with little education who had spent their lives roaming the Seven Seas. Ben's breed was chockful of superstition.

"I may be mistaken," Stan said slowly. "It may not be the mush-ice ghost. On the other hand— whoever heard of an ordinary human being walking naked about a ship in this climate?"

"Naked! How'd you know he was naked?"

"He was barefooted, anyway," Stan pointed out. "Look at the footprints. Are you sure you haven't heard the story of a sealer who—who broke his

leg, and was left on the ice by his shipmates?"
Stan's imagination was working overtime, and
he went on breathlessly. "They made a search for
him afterwards—but he'd gone. Ever since, he's
paid a visit to the sealing fleet each season."

"He's—— Here, what do you mean?" old Ben
was struggling hard not to believe, but the
superstitious part of his mind wanted all the
details.

"I don't mean the man has visited the sealing
fleet," Stan hastily corrected himself, "I mean his
ghost has. They tell me that when he knew his
shipmates were going to leave him, he swore he'd
have his revenge. And he has. He takes one man
off a ship each season. He visits every ship—naked
—and the first man to see him, or report seeing
him, is doomed."

"Doomed? You mean he dies?"

"That's right. The first chap who reports seeing
him never goes home." Then, with a shrug and
a casual wave of his hand, Stan went on: "Mind
you, I don't say it's true. You go and report these
footprints and put yourself in the clear with
Thorson. I'll tell you this, though; I'm saying
nothing. I'm taking no chances. Have you noticed
anything peculiar about these footprints?"

Ben looked down, and the longer he stared at
the incriminating blotches of oil, the more
worried he became.

"I only noticed the prints," he finally admitted.

"Hm! Well, I noticed something," Stan snorted.

"They *only came into the cabin*. There's no prints going out, is there? If my visitor was an ordinary chap, he must still be in the cabin. You'd better come and see who it is."

Stan was bluffing. If the old cook decided to make a search of the cabin the game was up.

Stan stood aside as if insisting Ben should re-enter the cabin, but the old man did not move.

"I've never heard tell o' this ghost," he muttered. "You'd think I'd have heard summat."

"Well, go and report the matter, then," Stan said crisply, "and if you give me your name and address I'll see that your relatives are told the moment I get home."

"Relatives! Told! What the devil are you talking about?" The suspicion in Ben's voice had now been superseded by something like angry fear. "You talk as if I were dying."

"I'm only going off what has happened before," Stan snapped. "I've told you the story—the first fellow who reports sign of the mush-ice ghost never goes home. I've warned you; but it's none of my business. You saw it first." With that he walked back into the cabin, and waited. His heart was thumping. On Ben's decision in the next few seconds depended what happened to Tubby Fenner.

A full minute went by before old Ben came into the cabin. He was scratching his stubbly chin.

"Look, mister," he began awkwardly, "I never were one for lookin' for trouble. If you're willin' to keep quiet about them footprints, I'll mop 'em up, and that'll be that."

"It makes no difference to me," Stan said carelessly, hiding his joy. "But if you want to keep it quiet, all right. After all, we're both Britishers."

"Aye, we are," Ben seemed to gather some consolation from that remark. "Funny I never heard o' this ghost. You'd have thought I would, wouldn't you?"

"People don't talk about it," Stan assured him, and then as an idea struck him, he went on: "You ask the fo'castle gang if they've heard about it. I'll bet they say they haven't. Sealers don't like talking about the ghost."

"Oh, they'll act dumb," Ben snorted. "A lousy bunch of Finns, Lapps, Poles—and a couple of Scowegians. Stinkin' tribe, they are," and with that he went off.

Stan stood for a moment by the table, then sat down. The reaction set in, and he quivered from head to foot. It seemed incredible that old Ben had really swallowed the cock-and-bull story that he, Stan Farrager, had made up on the spur of the moment.

Yet a minute or so later there was the clank of a bucket in the alley. Ben had returned to mop up the oil stains.

When he had gone Tubby crawled from beneath the bunk. His face was one huge grin, and he held out his right hand.

"Put it there, Stan. Cripes, I read a book once

by a chap named Baron Munchausen. The biggest
liar in the world, he was. You've got him beat.
Mush-ice ghost! Where'd you pick up that yarn?"

"I didn't," Stan managed a chuckle, "I made it
up. Good, eh?"

"You want to get one of them typewriters, man,
when you get home. You'd make a fortune, writ-
ing stories. My blinkin' hair was on end."

"Pull my other leg!" Stan poured coffee into a
cup. "Here! Have a swig. We'll have to drink
in turns."

It was while they were eating the breakfast
brought for Stan, that Tubby first saw the
possibilities of the "ghost."

"If the cook does tell the fo'castle gang," he
began, "I can see a chance for us. These Finns
are as superstitious as old wimmen. They'll
believe the yarn."

"Well, what good does it do us?" Stan asked.
"I wondered if it might be useful, but now that
I think about it, I can't see how we can use the
' ghost.'"

"You are looking at the ' ghost ' right now,"
Tubby said firmly, "and I'm going to haunt
somebody . . . and soon."

"Will it do any good?" Stan queried, and Tubby
snorted indignantly.

" Will it! Cripes, we'll have to do something.
Do you imagine Thorson will let us go free when
he's finished his pirate-chief act? Not on your
life."

With a piece of toast half-way to his mouth, Stan paused.

"Do you think he'd——" he began, and Tubby snorted again.

"Think! Use your loaf, boy, use your loaf. I don't know if piracy is a hanging matter to-day, but Thorson daren't let us go free. Don't you see what's going to happen? He's got his ship disguised as a Russian patrol vessel. Okay . . . he starts stopping sealers and confiscating their catches. What are they going to do? Sit down and smile? Not on your life."

Stan nodded and stared into space. Tubby, usually bubbling over with fun, was serious enough now as he tapped his friend on the arm and went on:

"What Thorson's going to do might even start a war. Can't you see? Diplomatic notes of protest from Norway, Sweden, all the governments whose sealing ships are robbed. Right . . . what does the Soviet Union do? They know they are innocent, so they reckon the other governments are just looking for an excuse for trouble."

"Yes," Stan admitted, "I hadn't thought of that. Thorson *must* be crazy, and you are right. He *won't* let us go. He can't."

Before Stan could say anything more, Tubby dropped to his knees and was under the bunk in a flash. Someone was coming.

A few moments later a deckhand entered the cabin with a command from Captain Thorson.

The *Bear* would be weighing anchor in a minute or so. Stan was to report to the engine-room at once.

"I'll think something up while you're away," Tubby promised, and with that Stan left the cabin.

Fifteen minutes later the *Bear* was edging her way cautiously out of the quiet anchorage and into the open sea. Standing in the wheelhouse, Thorson gave several sharp tugs at the siren cord, sending a shrill "cock-a-doodle-doo" into the thin, cold air.

"That's good-bye to Mr. Fenner," he chuckled, nudging Jimmy Staton in the ribs. "I hope he keeps warm at night."

CHAPTER FIVE

TUBBY HAS AN IDEA

FOR the next forty-eight hours the scene changed slowly. Heading east by south-east, the *Bear* kept just out of sight of the Murmansk coast. She passed only one small sealing vessel which had been having engine trouble. The remainder of the fleet, plodders and ten-knotters, had gone ahead while the *Bear* had been camouflaged from yacht to gunboat.

Under a leaden sky the *Bear* began to nose through mush-ice. At first it was thin, porridgy stuff, floating here and there in patches of varying size. Grey in colour—it looked more like unhealthy scum than ice.

Gradually, however, the porridge thickened, and definite floes could be seen. These, in turn, became fields, and the *Bear's* off-duty men in the fo'castle, slept or talked in an atmosphere of grinding and scraping as the slim bows ground through ice-floes. Occasionally when a watery sun broke through the clouds, the glare from the ice-fields was dazzling.

Stan saw his first seal on the second day. It was a pup, looking more innocent and harmless than any creature he had known. Its eyes were wide and babyish, while its curly fur gave it a toyshop appearance. That it had never encountered men or ships before was evident, for it was absolutely unafraid. The *Bear* passed within a biscuit toss of it and one of the Finnish gunners came on deck with a rifle. He would have shot it out of hand had not Thorson looked down from the bridge wing and stopped him.

"We are not here to shoot seals, you fool," he yelled, speaking Finnish with hardly a trace of accent. "We'll get our catch the easy way."

Sometime during the second night Thorson steered his craft over the imaginary line drawn by the Soviet Union between Cape Orloff and the northern tip of the Kanin Peninsula. He was now in forbidden territory, claimed by the Russians as their territorial waters. Close at hand was Morzhovets Island, with its tall look-out tower and its powerful wireless station.

Morzhovets Island was manned for the sole purpose of keeping sealers at bay, for within the precincts of the White Sea there gathered every year the greatest conglomeration of seals the world knows. Seals by the hundred thousand; seals so thick a gunner need hardly aim his rifle to make sure of a kill. It was the dream of every sealing captain to get into the White Sea some time. It would mean riches undreamed of. The watchers on Morzhovets Island, plus a three thousand ton war vessel, was the Soviet answer to such dreams, Poaching was risky.

Tubby and Stan discussed the position on the second night, after Ben had informed them that the *Bear* was within the forbidden zone. The *Bear* hove-to soon after midnight in a lane clear of ice, and with the exception of a watchman, all hands were given permission to turn in.

When the ship was quiet Tubby outlined his plan.

"It's now or never, man," he insisted, "and it might as well be now. I'll get the radio man out of his cabin. I'll give him a dose of Tubby Fenner's famous sleeping mixture," he demonstrated with clenched fists what he meant, "then we'll send out an S O S. You know morse. If we can just send out a warning, Thorson is as good as done for."

"Always assuming the set is powerful enough to send any distance," Stan pointed out, though he agreed with Tubby that a radioed S O S seemed to offer their only chance.

"It'll be strong enough," Tubby was bursting with confidence. "There'll be some British trawlers fishing off the Murmansk coast, and even if they missed it, I'll bet it'd be picked up by some of the Icelandic trawlers."

"Yes, but how do we get the radio man out of the way?" Stan wanted everything cut and dried before they started. He knew Tubby. The Geordie was like a bull in a china-shop and apt to overlook possible snags. "Don't forget, even if we get a message off, we're still stuck here. Short of killing the radio man, how are you going to keep him quiet?"

Tubby tapped his forehead significantly, and winked.

"If you are ever looking for a man wi' brains, Stan, you can't go wrong if you take a trip to Tyneside. We're born wi' brains up there, born wi' 'em. Now, listen."

Stan smiled, and listened.

"That bloke will be sitting comfortable as you please in his cabin," Tubby went on, "I knock on the door. He probably yells for me to come in. I just stands there waiting. If he doesn't come out I keep on knocking till he does. When he does I hit him, see? One on the beano with my left, and a quick follow up with the right. We carts him in and then you sends off the message. Simple."

"Hm! What about afterwards?" Stan asked. "He'll raise the alarm."

"He won't," Tubby was enjoying himself. "While you've been on duty in the engine-room, I've been doin' some thinkin'. The cook told the story of the mush-ice ghost to the fo'castle hands, didn't he?"

"Yes," Stan agreed, "but he said nobody seemed to have heard the yarn before."

"You can bet your last shirt button they've talked about it since," Tubby growled. "I know these fo'castle scum. Packed to the ears wi' superstition. So, when we've finished our job in the radio room we make it look as if it was the ghost what knocked him out, see?"

"What? Do you mean another oily footprint on the floor?" Stan was frowning at the idea.

"Will you let me finish?" Tubby demanded fiercely, though there was a twinkle in his deep blue eyes. "I'm beginning to wonder which of us two is the chief engineer and which is the 'Second.'"

"Sorry!"

"Apology accepted." Tubby was now grinning delightedly. "We put oily footprints on the radio-man's table. Across his papers, see. Nobody's going to miss those, eh? Not likely!"

It was a plan with lots of holes in it, yet Stan could think of nothing better. One thing they were both agreed upon—the urgent necessity of getting off a radio message to inform the outside world what was pending. If Thorson's piracy got under way, there was no telling to what it might lead. The most damaging feature was the fact that he would commit these piratical acts under the guise of a Russian man o' war.

Stan pounced on one snag. They were without oil to make the necessary ghostly footprints on the radio-man's table.

Tubby smiled in superior fashion. From beneath the bunk he produced a slip of greasy paper. It contained a small pat of butter.

"When I plan a thing, Stan, I plans down to the last little detail," he announced proudly. "I've been saving this butter during the past four meals. There should be enough; I haven't big feet."

Stan burst out laughing at that, and looked down appraisingly at Tubby's size eleven boots.

"If those aren't big feet, Tubby, I hope I never meet any one with outsize boots. Why, man, the butter needed to grease your feet would keep a family of ten in buttered bread for a month. Anyway, come on!"

"Lead on," Tubby urged, pocketing the small slab of butter, "I'm just itching to hit somebody. This sitting about, doing nothing, is no good for Mrs. Fenner's son."

A thin wind was whining through the ice-crusted rigging. The wireless aerials were lowered every few hours to keep them clear of ice, but the ordinary rigging was inches thick with ice.

The cold stung the cheeks like a knife, and there was a restless murmur from the ice-fields. Ice lanes were constantly freezing over, but the motion of the ice slabs moved by the wind kept breaking the new formed ice. The air thrilled to a constant thin chittering. Ice freezing, breaking, freezing and breaking again.

Brilliant stars looked down from a cloudless sky, while the pale fingers of Aurora Borealis played like phantom spokes in a ghostly wheel on the northern horizon. It was a night for warm cabins, and sleep.

Stan and Tubby crept along the deck, ready to melt into the darkness should the deck-watch appear. He however, must have been curled up in some protected spot, having a smoke, or maybe sitting in the cook's galley with a pint of coffee, and one of the sweet loaves of bread beloved of the Finns, for he was not seen at all.

Quietly Stan was helped on top of the cabins. Just as quietly he gave Tubby a hand. It was tricky work, for the metal had a sheathing of frozen spray, and was treacherous in the extreme.

Tiptoeing across the icy surface the two Britishers reached the dummy funnel. Not a sound was to be heard save the low drumming made by the wind on the funnel stays.

"Maybe they don't keep a man on watch at night," Stan suggested.

"If they don't," was Tubby's retort, "then we've had it, for I can't see 'em leaving the cabin unlocked. Thorson wouldn't trust his own mother. He's the kind what takes pennies off a blind beggar's plate. Stand aside, I'm going to knock."

Tubby rapped authoritatively on the metal door. The sound seemed to ring out like a bell, and Stan wondered uneasily if the deck watch would hear it. There was no response to the first knock. Tubby knocked again, the sort of knock a policeman, or a postman might use.

This brought an immediate response. From within the cabin came a faint reply, in Finnish, inviting them to enter.

Tubby waited a few moments, then knocked again. He stepped back half a pace, spat on his

left palm, rubbed the knuckles of his right fist
slowly across the wet spot, and grinned. The big
Geordie loved a fight, and the prospect of a rough-
house, even if it lasted only a few minutes, was
something which always pleased him immensely.

He was just about to rap on the door again
when the handle was turned, and the door pushed
open. Like most outside doors on ships, the door
in the funnel opened outwards. Because of this
outward opening the radio-man had to step
outside to see who was knocking.

Even so, Tubby was almost caught off-guard.
He had expected the radio-man to be outlined in
light from the cabin, being unaware of Thorson's
stringent orders regarding black-out aboard.
With the *Bear* in prohibited waters, a light might
be seen by a Russian patrol ship. Remembering
this the radio-man had obediently switched off
his light.

Stepping over the high sill the man looked out,
calling angrily.

Then Tubby hit him.

It was not one of Tubby's best punches, and in
other circumstances might not have been a perfect
knock-out punch. The clenched fist took the
Finnish radio-man high on the temple, instead of
just under the ear, but as it banged his head hard
against the iron door, the effect was just the same.
Tubby caught the man as he collapsed.

"Okay, Stan. Come on, the job's a good 'un,"
and hefting the unconscious man under his right

arm as if he had been a half-filled sack of chaff, Tubby stepped over the sill into the wireless room.

Stan followed, closed the door, then felt for his matches. The funnel wireless room, having no windows, was in utter darkness.

"Just like being down a coal mine," Tubby muttered. "Strike a light, Stan, then I can put this coon down."

Click!

Before Stan could strike a match there was a sudden flash of light which left both Britishers blinking. It was a moment or so before their eyes became accustomed to the brightness of the electric light. Then they saw the man who had switched it on.

"Cor!" Tubby whispered, and allowed the limp radio-man to slip to the floor. Stan said nothing, but he stared at the man who now held an automatic pistol levelled at him. It was Jimmy Staton.

Throughout all their careful planning, neither Tubby nor Stan had ever considered the possibility of two men in the wireless room.

If Tubby and Stan were momentarily demoralised, however, Jimmy Staton was equally amazed. Up to that moment he had been under the impression that Tubby was several hundred miles to the west, marooned on an unfriendly beach.

Staton broke the silence.

"What the devil are you doing here, Fenner? I thought we'd left you behind two days ago."

"I couldn't bear to let you go on without me," Tubby mocked. "I knew you'd need me before long, and . . ."

"Get back!" Staton warned, as Tubby began to inch forward a little. "I shouldn't miss at this range, and you're not exactly a small target."

"Just getting comfortable," Tubby murmured, but he ceased his forward movement.

Then Stan moved. He just stepped forward quietly, ignoring a warning jerk of Staton's gun, and seated himself at the radio table.

"Get up," Staton snapped. "What do you think you are doing?"

"I'm going to send out a message," Stan said, reaching out to the tuning dial.

"Take your hand away, Farrager, or I'll plug you." There was a snarl in Staton's voice. "I'll not warn you again."

Stan began to turn the wave-length dial, slowly but surely.

CHAPTER SIX

AN "S O S"

TUBBY FENNER looked unhappily at Staton, then at Stan. The two young men were about the same age, height, build and colouring. One, however, had furiously angry eyes, and an automatic. The other was calm and quietly defiant. Tubby dared do nothing, for Jimmy Staton would fire at the first movement.

"Stan," Tubby whispered, and was answered by the merest shake of the head.

Tubby closed his eyes. He had never felt so utterly helpless. A move would bring a bullet, and at that short range it was almost impossible to miss.

Stan broke the tension. Half-turning he asked:

" Have you the time, Tubby? I want to make sure the maximum number of people will be listening-in. And if . . ."

"You're not sending a word," Staton cut in harshly. "If you touch that set again, Stan Farrager, I'll shoot. I don't want to, but I shall. Now—get out of that chair."

Stan ignored him.

"The time, Tubby?"

" It's almost one-forty-five," Staton said coldly, "the middle of the Graveyard Watch. Stan, I'd hate to shoot you, but——"

Stan ignored him completely.

"Quarter to . . . that's fine. I've never forgotten a visit to the old Scoutroom of a chap who was a radio-op. on a liner. He told us that twice in every hour there's a close-down of commercial wireless, while men listen-in for S O S signals. There's a special wavelength for it. Six hundred metres, Jimmy?"

"Stop fooling," Staton snarled, and came a little nearer. "Listen, you always were pig-headed, Stan, but if you touch that morse key I'll have to shoot. Now. Get out of that chair!"

Stan looked his one-time friend squarely in the eyes.

"Jimmy, I'm going to send a message. If you want to shoot . . . all right. But before you shoot, just think: one of us is right. Is it me or you?"

"I'm not listening," Staton said savagely. "I'm in this racket up to the ears and if you get a message out, it means finish for us. I'm not having that. I've had a raw deal once, and now I'm out for easy money. Get out of that chair!"

"That isn't like you, Jim," Stan said soberly.

"Stop preaching," Staton snarled, "and get out of that chair!"

"It *was* six hundred metres, wasn't it, Tubby?"

Stan half-turned to Tubby Fenner, while his hand strayed to the tuning dial.

"Get your hand away from that dial!"

Stan turned and looked at Staton again. Then in a very quiet voice he said:

"If you want to stop me, Jimmy, you'll have to shoot. I'm going to use the radio."

Perspiration was trickling down Tubby Fenner's cheeks while the short hairs on the back of his neck were prickling with apprehension. Both these men were determined, and unless one of them caved in, Stan Farrager would be either dead or badly wounded in the next few seconds.

Stan began to turn the dial controlling the set-tuning; slowly the dial moved round . . . seven hundred metres, six-eighty . . . six-fifty . . . six-thirty-five. Tubby watched out of the corner of his eye for the flash of Staton's gun.

Stan moved his hand a little. The set was at six hundred metres . . . the universal waveband adopted for SOS messages. It was a strangely moving thought that throughout the northern waters, at that moment, scores of men on scores of ships would be doing exactly what Stan Farrager had just done. They would have changed over from commercial wavebands. Every working set would be on six hundred metres. Men would be seated at the big desks aboard palatial liners, in cubby holes aboard freighters, aboard rusty tramps, possibly even on small coasting vessels. For a few minutes they would listen in on a

radio silence . . . a silence made specially for
S O S messages. If Stan could get his message
tapped out, then it was ten to one someone would
hear him.

Tubby came back to earth with a jump. Stan
had depressed a small black knob, and a tiny pilot
light glowed. The set was "live." For the last
time, Jimmy Staton whispered a warning: "I
shall shoot."

Jimmy Staton was not bluffing.

Stan nodded and said: "If you shoot me,
Jimmy, you'll never forget it. We were pals once.
Pals! Could you shoot me?"

Staton was silent; but the gun quivered as if
the finger was tightening on the trigger.

"Don't do it," Staton pleaded, and to Tubby
there was more menace in that plea than in
Staton's threats. Tubby knew for certain, then,
that Jimmy Staton would shoot.

Stan's hand moved. The first three dots of the
S O S pulsed out through the ether, then . . .

Bang!

The automatic belched flame, and the report in
that confined space was like the clap of a thunder-
bolt. For a few moments the radio cabin was a
howling bedlam of sound. The bullet was
smashed out of shape and ricocheted from one
point to another, striking sparks and whining
fiendishly before dropping to the floor.

Stan Farrager remained like a statue, his right
hand poised on the morse-key. The flash of the

gun had been so close that, for the moment, he was too shocked to think.

Tubby Fenner ducked instinctively, then came to life as Jimmy Staton moved. Staton was angry with himself for lifting the muzzle of his automatic at the very last moment, thus sending the bullet harmlessly over Stan's shoulder. He swung the weapon, meaning to bring it down on Stan's head.

"You asked for it, you f—— Oh!"

His howl of pain came when Tubby Fenner thrust out his brawny right arm in a parrying stroke. Tubby saved Stan from a blow which would have laid him unconscious across the table.

The shock, as Staton's wrist came down on the Geordie's rock-like arm sent the automatic flying. Off balance, Staton reeled across the table, and Tubby brought round a left hook which smashed Staton sideways. He hit the wall, then tumbled to the floor, where he sat gaping, too dazed to do anything but blink.

"Thanks." There was a quiver in Stan's voice as he held out the automatic which had dropped near his hand. "Here, you'd better have the gun. I can't wait any longer. The S O S time will soon be over now, and I can't send quickly."

Stan laid a shaking hand on the morse-key, Jimmy Staton made to scramble to his feet, but he relaxed as Tubby threatened him with the gun.

"Don't do it, Stan," Staton pleaded. "You'll ruin everything. Listen. Long before any British ship could get here there'd be a Russian warship on to us. They've got a wireless station on Morzhovets Island. They've a bunch of trained operators there who speak every major language. If you send an S O S they'll put every available patrol ship on to us. They'd have us before sundown to-morrow. Stan—have you ever been in a Soviet prison? It'll be hell if we're caught, and death for me. I know it will."

Stan said nothing. The morse-key went up and down. Three dots, three dashes, three dots . . . repeated several times. Whoever heard that dread signal would hang on for what followed, even if the normal S O S radio silence was ended.

Painstakingly he told the story of what Thorson planned; asking for the message to be relayed to the British Government at once. Then he gave the position of the ship. He could give neither latitude nor longitude, but he knew they were several hours steaming south of the Kanin Peninsula . . . inside the neck of water leading to the White Sea.

In the middle of repeating this there was a sudden flash, and the set went dead. Jimmy Staton had jerked out the leads which brought current from the engine-room. Without power the radio was useless.

"Now, what?" Staton demanded.

"I've given our position," Stan said, rising from

his chair. "If the Russians on Morzhovets Island got it *they'll* put a spoke in Thorson's wheel—that's the main thing. Now, you can go and warn Thorson."

Turning to Tubby he said:

"Give him his gun. I don't believe in shooting. In any case, one gun is no use."

"But we——" Tubby began, then regretfully tossed the automatic to Staton. "There you are, mister. If you'll take my advice you'll chuck the thing away. Guns always get folk into trouble."

Staton got to his feet. For a moment he stood silently caressing his face; it was already showing signs of an ugly bruise. When Tubby punched any one he left his mark.

"We'll go," Stan turned away, but stopped as Staton said:

"Wait a minute Stan." Staton's voice had a queer huskiness about it. "What are you going to do about Stanislaw?"

"Who?" Stan and Tubby voice the question together.

"The wireless man. When he regains consciousness he'll report this. If Thorson finds out what you've done he'll kill you." That last sentence had a convincing ring, as if Staton was telling the truth, nothing more and nothing less.

"You've got something on your mind?" Tubby asked. "You're not warning us out of any love for Stan. If you've got any ideas . . . out with 'em. That fellow's showing signs of coming round."

Staton glared angrily at the Geordie, then sneered:

"You know *all* the answers, don't you Anyway, I *am* thinking about myself. Listen. Keep quiet over this business, and I'll do the same. Stanislaw won't know who hit him, or what hit him. He probably won't remember anything about it. I'll swear I wasn't in the cabin with him when you came. What do you say?"

"That's a bit more like the old Jimmy," Stan said smiling, but Staton merely curled his lip derisively.

"Cut that out. I'm not turning over any new leaves. I'm looking after myself—I don't want Thorson to know you got the better of me. Now, is it a bargain?"

"We've nothing to lose," Tubby agreed.

"Okay, we'll put Stanislaw in his chair, and let him think what he likes. He'll kick up a howl, but what happens——"

"Here, wait a minute." Stan had suddenly remembered something. "We can quieten him, *and* rouse no suspicions."

"How?"

"You leave it to us, Jimmy," Stan urged, and as Staton still hesitated, frankly suspicious, he went on: "Look, we're not thinking of trying to repair the wireless set."

"I'll stay and watch, just the same," Staton's suspicions were not allayed in the least. "You knew how to send an S O S, didn't you?"

"Oh, all right," Stan turned to Tubby. "Got the butter?"

Tubby gaped, then grinned. He handed over the small packet of butter then doffed his shoes and stockings.

Taking a message pad, Stan tore out several sheets, scattering them haphazardly across the table. Then, with Staton watching closely, Stan carefully smeared Tubby's bare feet with butter, rubbing the stuff on with a slip of paper so that no part was missed, and no part had other than a greasy film.

Gingerly, Tubby got on to the table, and carefully put the greasy imprints of his big feet on the papers, Stan holding them down so that they would not adhere to the Geordie's soles.

"I don't get this," Staton was puzzled. "What's it all about?"

Tubby ignored him, and wiping his feet clean, hastily put on his shoes and stockings again.

"What you don't know won't hurt you, Jimmy," Stan said soberly, "but what we've just done *may* keep the wireless man quiet. If it doesn't—well, that's too bad for us. Here, give me a hand. We'll sit him at the table. He's definitely beginning to come round."

They propped the still dazed Stanislaw in his

chair, his crossed arms on the table, his forehead resting on the leather table covering. Then they left the cabin and carefully closed the steel door behind them.

An icy wind was still blowing but no clouds darkened the starlit sky. Over in the north the Northern Lights flickered uneasily, pale lemon, tinged with ethereal blue and gauzy pink, unreal and fantastically beautiful.

Before they parted Stan turned to Jimmy and said quietly:

"It's not too late to turn back, Jimmy. If you——"

Jimmy Staton laughed ironically.

"Sorry, you can't reform me, Stan. I've said good-bye to that kind of thing," and he moved aft.

Stan and Tubby hurried back to their cabin. If Staton had not been on hand to complicate matters they might possibly have received a reply to their S O S. As it was, they did not know whether it had been picked up or not. And there was Stanislaw to worry about.

While they were discussing things there was activity on Morzhovets Island, and aboard a three-thousand ton Russian patrol ship. One of the English speaking operators on Morzhovets had got Stan's message. Every word was written down including the *Bear*'s position. Then a direction-finding apparatus was put to work, and a line laid on the *Bear*.

Another operator had contacted the three-thousand ton patrol ship. She was not in time to get a cross-bearing on the *Bear*, but she was ordered to proceed at once, and make a search.

Less than nine sea miles separated the two craft when Stan and Tubby finally lay down to sleep.

CHAPTER SEVEN

THORSON RESISTS ARREST

IN THE wireless cabin of the *Bear* Stanislaw came round very slowly. When he finally lifted his head from the wireless table he stared vacantly before him, hands clasping aching temples. There was a lump the size of a pigeon egg on the right side of his head, a great bruise on his left temple where Tubby Fenner had hit him.

Finally Stanislaw focused his gaze on the table before him. Then he noticed the papers bearing two greasy footprints. Tubby had made them for his special benefit.

Stanislaw had heard the cook tell the story of the mush-ice ghost. He had listened in silence to the tale of the naked man who boarded sealing ships, and left imprints of oily feet as a warning that he meant to bring death to one of the crew. The crew of the *Bear*, mostly Finns and Lapps, were very superstitious men and never once doubted the authenticity of the "ghost" story.

The wireless man's face had been pallid enough before he saw the greasy footprints, but it went even paler at the sight of the unmistakable evidence of a visit from the mush-ice ghost. Not for a moment did he doubt the identity of his attacker.

Gripped by superstitious fear he stumbled to the door, and staggered out on to the ice-covered plates. He moved too quickly, slipped, and slithering to the edge of the cabin roof, dropped with a crash to the deck.

In the cook's galley the deck watch was passing the bitterly cold hours with a pint mug of coffee and a long curved pipe.

He heard the crash, looked up, hesitated, then went out to investigate. Falling over the wireless man, he carried him to the galley; then went back, for he had noticed the light shining from the wireless cabin . . . the door was open, the light still switched on.

"I smell trouble," he muttered, and was making his way cautiously along the top of the cabins when he thought he saw a light over to the west.

Shading his eyes he stared anxiously. All was dark, and he was just deciding he had been mistaken when the light reappeared. It was a searchlight, and the pale beam moved slowly over the ice-fields until it reached the *Bear*. It swept gently past her, hesitated, then turned back. Keen eyes had picked out the black hulk of the ship against the white of the ice-field.

For a moment the deck watch stood petrified, then he gave a yell—a frightened yell. In that forbidden area a searchlight could have only one meaning: a Russian patrol ship.

Within a minute of the alarm being given, the *Bear* was like an overturned ant's nest, though there was order in the apparent confusion. Thorson had drilled his men well, and each knew exactly what he had to do in case of an emergency.

One man came to call Stan Farrager, and Tubby Fenner performed a miracle of legerdemain. He vanished. For a man of his bulk it was startling the way he shot under the bunk, but even so he was barely in time.

Flinging open the cabin door the seaman yelled: "Report to the engine-room at once. Captain Thorson's orders!" Then he raced off again.

"By hooky, Stan, there's a Russian coming," Tubby said. "That's the answer from Morzhovets Island already."

Stan nodded and dressed at a speed which would have made a first-class fireman go green with envy.

"Better keep out of sight," he warned, then he was off, racing for the engine-room. He could hear the jangle of the engine-room signal bells, and even as he clattered down the ladder the diesels were beginning to turn over under the impulse of the compressed air starters. Thorson always had one man on duty down below, night and day.

As Stan raced along the deck, he had seen two things. One was a dazzling white *eye*, the Russian's searchlight, and the other was a much smaller spot of light, the latter winking away in the manner peculiar to morse signal lamps.

The Russian signaller was ordering the *Bear* to prepare to receive a boarding party.

Before his feet touched the engine-room plates, Stan was looking across at the indicator, and was surprised to see it showing merely "Stand by engines."

"He'll never get away now," Stan decided, and moved to the controls to nurse the unevenly thumping diesels into a smooth warm-up. If Thorson tried to get away he would need every ounce of power the engines could give.

While Stan was busy below, the apparent confusion on deck had sorted itself out. A gun-crew was squatting by the Bofors gun in the bows. The gun was loaded, and the men kept down out of sight.

The bridge, armoured as had been ship's bridges during war-time, had only the starboard observation shutter open. Short of a direct hit from a three or four-inch shell, the men in the wheelhouse were safe.

Lining the starboard rail, but keeping below rail level, were a dozen riflemen, each with a heavy rifle. Every man was a picked marksman.

The Russian was closing in, and to the men aboard her it must have seemed as if the *Bear* was deserted. She remained still, and without sign of life.

Then, from the wheelhouse, Thorson yelled a command:

"Fire!"

Like puppets working on a single string, the twelve marksmen popped over the rail, levelled their rifles, and fired a volley. A moment later the *Bear* was in darkness. That volley had been aimed at the searchlight.

Within seconds, however, another searchlight came to life. Thorson gave his fire order once more, and the second light was put out just as quickly.

Down below, bells jangled, and the engine-room indicator swung round to " Full speed astern."

Stan flicked the handle of his indicator over to show he had got the order, then he opened up. The *Bear* began to tremble; the water at her stern boiled as the twin screws raced for a moment before settling down to the business of moving the ship astern.

As soon as he was sure everything was going right, Stan raced for the deck, leaving the greaser at the controls. In normal circumstances he would never have left his post. Under Thorson, however, he felt no compunction, and wanted to see what was happening. If the Russian showed her teeth, as she might well do, a shell to stop the *Bear* might hit the engine-room. Stan had no desire to be down below when that happened.

The *Bear* was beginning to move, but it seemed as if the captain of the Russian ship had second sight. He had altered course a little, and was heading directly for the *Bear,* on a course which must bring disaster to the lighter vessel.

There were no lights on the Russian now. Even the morse lamp had ceased its staccato blinking; but in the starlight, reflected wanly from the snow and ice, it was possible to make out the Russian ship as a vague shape, hurtling through hummock and ice-cake with a fine disregard for anything. The air quivered with the smash and chitter of ice, and the surging roar of powerful engines.

If she hit the *Bear* it would be the end for most of them. The Russians vastly superior weight, and armour, would push the lighter vessel over and under, or cut her clean in two.

Thinking to warn Tubby, Stan turned to run, but a strong hand grabbed him, and Tubby whispered urgently:

"Hold your hosses. Stan!"

"Was just coming to warn you," and at that Tubby laughed.

"I never stay a-bed when there's trouble brewing. Lor, come on, stern-side for us, man!" Tubby ordered. "We've had it."

"It's Thorson's fault," Stan snapped. "If he'd started half a minute earlier we'd have got clear," and with that he braced himself for the shock. The Russian seemed suddenly to have increased speed . . . it was actually an optical illusion, due to the fact that the *Bear* was drawing steadily astern, bringing her foe more for'ard.

"Hold it—hold it," Tubby warned, and they both crouched, steadying themselves for the crash.

The two shadows merged—but there was no shock; no scream of twisted metal, no crunch of shattering steel plates. The *Bear* continued to slide backwards with gradually increasing speed, while the larger shadow swept across her bows.

"Holy smoke, she's missed us," Tubby gasped. As he spoke the darkness was suddenly broken by a continuous stabbing of light flashes as twin machine-guns began to belch lead and flame.

For about thirty seconds the bridgework of the *Bear* was subjected to a terrific hammering, and bullets bounced off her light armour with a deafening noise, ricocheting in all directions. Then, as the Russian sped on into the darkness, the firing ceased.

Thorson gave another crisp, monosyllabic command.

The crew of the Bofors gun came to life, and in an incredibly short time were pumping shells after the Russian. Four shots hit her, each signalled by a sudden burst of flame, followed by the cracking report of the explosion.

"Well!" Stan gasped. "If that isn't asking for trouble, I don't know what is."

"Cor, yes," Tubby agreed. "There isn't a naval man afloat would let that pass. He's already had his searchlights doused, and now Thorson has the cheek to fire on him with a—ha-ah—engine-room!"

Stan had heard the jangle of telegraph bells and he shot down the ladder like a terrified monkey.

The engine-room indicator had swung half-way round the board and now stood at "Full speed ahead."

"Answer him!" Stan yelled, forgetting that his greaser understood no English. The man, however, realised what was required, and while Stan reversed the screws the Pole made the bells in the wheelhouse clang again as he swung the indicator over to "Full speed ahead."

The *Bear* quivered as the screws threshed water, fighting to reverse the ship's astern movement. Then the *Bear* started to slide ahead, slowly at first, then with increasing speed.

Thorson's strategy was sound. The Russian had to make a half circle before he could line up with the *Bear* again, and now, with both search-lights out of action, he was blind.

With his diesels at full stretch Thorson raced north, and when the first grey light of morning began to disperse the gloom he had steered his ship out past the Kanin Peninsula, and so into international waters. There, in theory, he was safe, since it is forbidden, except in time of war, for any ship to be stopped at sea unless it is within the three-mile limit of the nation to whom the warship belongs.

When they were safe, Thorson sent for Stan.

In the luxuriantly appointed stateroom, Thorson sat smoking a cheroot. For a moment he seemed lost in thought and took no notice of the Britisher.

Then he said something which made Stan's heart thump.

"What did you hit my wireless-man with, last night, Mr. Farrager? Surely it wasn't necessary to *kill him*?"

"Kill him!" Stan was caught off guard, and in horror he tried to defend himself. "He wasn't dead when——"

"So it *was* you." Thorson laughed, a quiet, satisfied laugh, and Stan could have kicked himself for being trapped so easily. Realising he had given himself away he sat down, making himself as comfortable as possible for what might come next.

Thorson continued to pull gently at his cheroot, blowing thin blue smoke into the air, and when he posed his next question there was a cynical smile on his face, which suggested he was saying: "I'm much too clever to be fooled by a simpleton like you."

Actually he asked:

"What size of boots do you take, Mr. Farrager. Put your feet out."

There was no question of refusing. Two armed men were standing by, and Stan put out his feet.

"That do?" he asked sarcastically.

"My crew are superstitious," Thorson said, staring hard at Stan's feet. "Mostly Finns and Lapps; quite uneducated; reeking with ghost stories and witchcraft yarns. About ten minutes ago they sent a deputation to see me, requesting that I sail the ship back to Tromso . . . as the mush-ice ghost was aboard."

"The mush——?" Stan tried not to look pleased. So the wireless man had talked about the "ghostly" attack on him. Stan could see the connection between Thorson's accusation regarding the wireless man, and his own size in shoes. Obviously the oily footprints on the wireless table had been seen. Stan took size six and a half shoes while Tubby's feet were at least elevens.

"Ever heard of the mush-ice ghost?" Thorson asked, and now there was no humour in his voice.

"I can't say I believe in ghosts," Stan replied, "but I'm not fool enough to say there aren't any."

"No man with a grain of common sense believes in ghosts," Thorson said curtly, "and no ghost ever made footprints like this." From another table he brought the sheets of paper on which Tubby Fenner had so carefully put his butter-smeared feet. The grease had spread so that now the footprints were terrific.

"I'm not suggesting you made that imprint," Thorson said coldly, "nor did any of my crew. Finns and Lapps are smallish men, with correspondingly small feet. In any case, I've had them all in here, before I sent for you."

"'Fraid I can't offer any suggestion," Stan gave a shrug, and pretended boredom.

Thorson nodded, then said:

"My suggestion, Farrager, is—we have somebody aboard who ought not to be here. There's only one person I can think of . . . who could be aboard. You know who I mean."

"Not being a thought reader, I'm afraid I don't."

Thorson sneered.

"Mr. Farrager, you were in the radio room last night; you admitted the fact. These footprints were not made by you so I can only assume you've got Fenner in your cabin."

"Don't be an idiot!" Stan snapped. "Where could he hide? The cook comes in regularly."

"For your sake, and his," Thorson said quietly, "I hope I am mistaken. That Russian ship did not come on us by chance. Someone used my radio last night. The wireless man tells me that the same someone also pulled out the power leads. You wouldn't know anything of that I suppose?" Without waiting for Stan to affirm or deny the allegation Thorson went on: "If Fenner is aboard he's due for a long cold swim. Come on. We'll go and see if he is where I think he is."

Stan was taken out on deck. The glare from the ice-floes made him blink, for a pale sun was shining. The *Bear* was slowly forcing her way through a field of broken ice, and somewhere ahead a thin plume of smoke suggested one of the bona fide sealers was at work.

Thorson must have read his thoughts, for he said:

"Don't worry, Mr. Farrager, I shan't put Fenner over the side in daylight. I wouldn't take a chance of him being picked up by any one, not even a Russian patrol ship."

"I'm not worrying," Stan tried to keep up his bluff, hoping against hope that Tubby might have left the cabin. Might even have found a hiding place among the oil storage tanks; anywhere but in the cabin.

Opening the cabin door, he stood aside to allow Thorson to enter. He wanted to give Tubby time to do something.

"After you," Thorson said, a mocking smile on his face.

Reluctantly Stan entered the cabin, and his hopes died. Tubby was sitting at the table quietly filling his pipe.

CHAPTER EIGHT

DEATH FOR TWO

THERE was no chance of fighting a way out. Two men blocked the way to the deck and each had an automatic.

Thorson, confident he held the whiphand, leaned against the cabin wall and stared across at Tubby Fenner, a sneering smile on his lean dark face.

"I underestimated you," he said slowly, while Tubby with supreme indifference, sucked steadily at his pipe, the flame leaping up, then disappearing back into the bowl. His calm was superb, and Stan wondered if he had some ace card up his sleeve.

"I didn't expect to see you so soon," Tubby finally admitted, holding the matchbox over his pipe bowl, and puffing quietly. "Sit down. As you are the host, I suppose it's only polite to offer you a chair. I'm afraid Stan will have to keep on his feet for once."

"I'm not sure that I haven't a sneaking admiration for you Britishers," Thorson said slowly. "Sometimes I think you are just plain stupid, and don't know when you are licked. Sometimes I wonder if you are much cleverer than you appear."

"I bet you didn't expect to see me again, eh?" Tubby asked, and his chuckle was as natural as if he were cracking a joke. Then, confidentially, he went on: "You know, I'm a lad as can't stand solitude. Besides, that oil stove you left me— cor, it stank worse than a shipload of dead codfish!"

"Get out of that chair!" Thorson suddenly lost his good humour. There was a dangerous glitter in his eyes, and the muscles of his cheeks were twitching. It upset him to see Tubby so un-perturbed.

Tubby raised his eyebrows, but did not move.

"Get out of here!" Thorson roared, and a command to the guards brought both men into the cabin on the run.

"I wouldn't do nothing rash if I was you," Tubby cautioned, and looked for a moment as if he contemplated tackling the two men, armed though they were. "I'm warning you, Thorson— I used your wireless last night. Maybe you didn't know that. It's a good set, and powerful. Strong enough to reach as far as the Icelandic fishing grounds. There's always trawlermen listening-in on the short waveband up there."

Thorson changed again. The glitter faded from his eyes, and he laughed.

"Go on, Mr. Fenner," he jeered, "I'm listening. It pays to listen."

"You're dead right, there, matey," Tubby agreed, and now he had dropped his air of indiffer-ence, and became the Tubby who was to be relied on in a tight corner. "I'm warning you. My message last night has cooked your goose. As far as this pirate stunt of yours is concerned, you've had it."

Thorson laughed softly.

"Go on—I like to hear you," he urged.

"That's something," Tubby said, and chuckled again, "I always reckoned I'd be a Radio Star one day, but I never thought it'd be over a caper like this. Anyway, I'll be serious."

"I appreciate that," Thorson sneered.

"Well, take my tip. Run us back to Tromso, and give yourself up, before the thing gets too sticky. You can't get away with it. I've spilled the beans—if you know what words like that mean?"

"Finished?"

"Just about," Tubby agreed, "and if you harm either me or Stan, you'll swing for it. And don't kid yourself you'll get away. They all think they're too clever to be caught. They always are, Thorson." And Tubby put a thick hand about his own throat to suggest the hangman's rope.

"Take him on deck," Thorson ordered, and now the glitter had come back to his eyes. "You talk too much, Mr. Fenner, and I have a way with talkers. When they've swallowed a certain amount of water, they don't talk any more, if you know what words like that mean," he ended, mimicking Tubby.

As Tubby walked out of the cabin Stan addressed Thorson.

"If you harm him," he said quietly, "don't count on me as an engineer. I'll go down to the diesels, but it will be to put them out of action."

For a moment it seemed as if Thorson would leap at Stan and tear him to pieces. He tensed and the veins in his neck swelled while his face darkened. His long fingers clenched and unclenched.

"You—you——" he spluttered, and swore vilely until gradually the fury left his face, as if the abuse had acted as a safety valve.

"Get down in the engine-room at once!" he said, when he had finally cooled off. "If ever you say anything like that——"

"You can't scare me," Stan interrupted, though he was quaking a little inwardly. "Your two greasers know nothing about diesels, Thorson. You need me. You can't manage without a skilled diesel man. Harm Tubby—and you might as well throw me overboard as well."

It was stalemate. The two seamen who had been escorting Tubby Fenner on deck, had stopped. Thorson turned and looked past them at the burly "Geordie." Tubby was still sucking quietly at his pipe.

"Aye, weigh it up careful-like," Tubby advised. "I've known Stan a long time. If he says he'll do a thing, you can bet your boots he'll do it."

Just then there was an urgent cry from the look-out in the crow's nest. Stan thought he detected a look of relief in Thorson's eyes, as if he were glad of the distraction, since it saved him from climbing down before his seamen.

"Engine-room," he snapped, glaring at Stan. Then, turning to Tubby, "You can stay here. I'll decide what to do, later."

"I go below only if Tubby comes," Stan said dourly. "Make your choice."

For a moment there was murder in Thorson's eyes, then he nodded.

"There's a Russian patrol ship coming for us," he said quietly. "Get below, both of you."

Stan joined Tubby on deck; they could see no sign of the approaching Russian, but ice hummocks, some of them eight and nine feet high, cut off the distant view.

A snarl from Thorson and they clattered down the ladder to the warmth of the engine-room.

The bells jangled for full speed ahead, and for three hours there was a chase, with the *Bear* at full stretch. Thorson took some terrible risks with his ship in order to gain time. His crew were stripping the camouflage from the *Bear*; taking off the iron sheeting which protected the bridge, removing the Bofors gun from the foredeck, and stowing it below in one of the oil tanks, specially prepared for such an emergency. The marks where machine-gun bullets had hit bridge, deck, and rails, were painted over and dirtied, so that it would need much more than a casual glance to reveal any scars. What had taken a couple of days to erect was removed in three hours.

Once or twice Stan, and then Tubby, went on deck to see how the chase was progressing. It was Tubby who brought the news that they were threading their way through the centre of the sealing fleet.

"Never seen such a ghastly business," Tubby said, disgust in his voice. "It's just mass murder. There are whole gangs of men out on the ice, killing seals right and left. Others are following them up, skinning the seals and leaving the carcases lying everywhere. It's just like a giant slaughter yard."

Stan went up to look for himself, but did not stay long. Remembering the pathetic innocence of the first seal pup he had seen a few days earlier, the sight was appalling. All this was going on so that women could have sealskin coats.

At the end of three hours the engine-room indicator spun round to 'Stop—finished with engines.'

The silence which followed was almost ghostly, with only the gentle purr of the lighting-set diesel as a soft undertone.

"We've had it," Stan muttered. "The Russian has been gaining on us all the time. Go and see what's happening Tubby. I'll stand by in case he wants us to start up again."

Tubby went up on deck, while Stan made a quick check-up on various vital points in the engine-room which could not be attended to while the engines were in motion.

Time passed, and Tubby did not reappear. Stan looked at his watch. Something had gone wrong! It was fifteen minutes since Tubby went on deck, and there was an unnatural quiet about everything. He climbed the ladder to deck level, and looked out. He half-expected to see the Russian patrol vessel hove-to within speaking distance; but his view was restricted by ice-hummocks. His first impression was that they were back where they had started, the scene was so similar.

Walking towards the stern he saw three men out on the ice. They were walking slowly along in single file, backs bent as they towed bundles of sealskins. They looked unutterably weary, far too weary even to glance across at the *Bear*. Of Tubby there was no sign, and the ship was strangely quiet. The sun was dipping low in the west, and dark clouds in the east told of approaching night.

Then Thorson stepped on to the bridge wing and called out:

"Ah, Mr. Farrager. I was going to send for you. Your friend has generously volunteered to help us, an offer I was glad to accept." Thorson winked as he said that, and was obviously pleased with himself. It confirmed Stan's presentiment that trouble was brewing. Walking towards the bridge he awaited Thorson's explanation.

"Fenner thought he would like to try his hand at sealing," Thorson went on, chuckling gleefully. "I told him he wouldn't like it, but he insisted on going. I fancy he imagined it would reduce his weight a little. Anyway I sent him out with two of my best gunners. They'll look after him."

Stan looked up for a moment, then said quietly:

"If he doesn't return, you'll never get this ship back to Tromso."

The threat was lost on Thorson, who laughed loudly.

"Now, now!" he mocked. "Let's not be silly. I had to get him out of the way. You must go sealing, too. Most of the men are out on the ice."

He moved out of sight, but a few moments later clattered down the bridge ladder to the deck.

"If you look about carefully, Mr. Farrager, you will see that our camouflage has been removed. We have, of necessity, become a bona fide sealer again. Do you know what the Russians are doing?"

Stan merely looked at him, and Thorson went on:

"They seem to be annoyed about last night, and they are breaking all the International Rules regarding shipping. They are boarding vessels outside their own territorial waters. Can you imagine it, eh? I wonder if they might be looking for someone with a Bofors gun."

"The smartest people overstep themselves," Stan snapped.

"Yes, I think the Russians are going too far," Thorson agreed, winking, and deliberately mis-understanding Stan, "but it is going to fit in with my plans very nicely. Once the Russians have searched us—I shall have my camouflage replaced. Then up goes the Russian flag, and when I go about the business of confiscating seal-skins from the fleet—there isn't a single man but will swear it was the Russians who did the thieving. Nobody could blame them for thinking that either. You don't look pleased, Mr. Farrager. You should rejoice with me—it augurs for a very successful trip for all aboard the *Bear*."

"You know what I think of you," Stan said firmly, "and I'm warning you again. If Tubby doesn't come back, it's going——"

"I'll give you something to take your mind off him," Thorson interrupted. "I'll give you a sealing knife, some knee boots, and a thick coat. You are going out on the ice for an hour or so. You see, that Russian patrol ship isn't very far away, and I want her to search us while you and Mr. Fenner are not here. Now . . . ah, here is Jimmee, and he's got your equipment."

Jimmy Staton had come on deck and was carrying knee boots, a heavy coat, a cap with thick earflaps, as well as a belt and knife.

"Better hide your own boots in the engine-room locker," Jimmy suggested, handing over the kit. "If the Russians see them, they might confiscate them. British leather is prized you know." He winked as he spoke and it was not a humorous wink, but one intended to convey a message.

What that message was Stan could not imagine, but he got the idea there was something in the engine-room for him. Otherwise why had Jimmy specifically mentioned the engine-room locker? He turned in silence and went through the doorway leading below.

Once down there he went across to the clothes locker. There were hooks and a small shelf. On that shelf was a scrap of paper. With puckered brows he deciphered the faint, and hurriedly scribbled words. There were five only, and no signature:

"You are not coming back."

Stan experienced the same kind of chilling fear which must come to any one who listens to a death sentence. "*You are not coming back.*" Tubby Fenner was already out on the ice, in company with two gunners. It was intended that he, Stan Farrager, should go the same way. Whether Thorson had ordered his two prisoners to be shot, or merely left out there to die, did not matter. The end planned was the same. They were not coming back.

"Well, Jimmy," he whispered, as he began to change into the knee-boots Jimmy Staton had given him, "you've warned me, but that isn't much use. If you'd given me a gun I might have had a chance."

Five minutes later, just as Stan was finishing a short note, Thorson yelled down to him, ordering him on deck at once.

"Coming!" Stan hastily signed the note and left it in a conspicuous place by the diesel controls,

Then he hurried on deck to be greeted by a volley of curses. Thorson was almost beside himself with fury. Pointing for'ard he drew Stan's attention to a vessel little more than half a mile away. It was impossible to tell what flag she flew, but by the way she was flinging ice from her bows, she was a heavy craft built for this kind of work. In that case there was little doubt she was the Russian patrol ship.

Ignoring ice-lanes the ice-breaker cum patrol-ship could plough her way across ice-fields which would hold fast any sealer, and she was coming across to search the *Bear* for evidence of the gun which had fired at her during the previous night.

"Over the side," Thorson roared, and Stan had no option but to obey. His two guards were dark-skinned Lapp gunners, each man carrying the traditional rifle and bag of cartridges. If they were intercepted for interrogation, they conformed in every way with the normal seal-gunner, while Stan would be taken for the skinner—his coat, boots, cap and knife-belt being positive identification.

"K. Y. P. D.!" Jimmy Staton yelled that cryptic message across the ice, some thirty seconds after Stan had begun to flounder along with his guards.

"K. Y. P. D.!" Stan turned at once. It was years since he had ever thought of that code-message, but its significance went home immediately. It was one of the so-called secret messages of the Scout Patrol of which he had been leader, and Jimmy Staton his second in command. It was a warning of impending trouble, and stood for: "Keep your powder dry."

'K. Y. P. D.' Stan looked at his two guards. They were taciturn to a degree, and one made an impatient gesture indicating that Stan should hurry.

Yes, hurry . . . hurry to his death, and so far as he could see there was nothing he could do about it. Stan fell into line with his guards, his face grim.

CHAPTER NINE

AN ACE CARD

FOR ten minutes Stan Farrager and his Lapp guards marched away from the *Bear*. The Lapps never looked back. Years in the ice-fields made it second nature for them to find their way back to the ship with ease. Stan, who had never before been on mush-ice, realised how easy it would be for him to get lost. There were no signposts . . . nothing but ice and water.

At the end of five minutes he decided he must make an attempt to escape at once, or he was finished. The sun had gone, leaving only a pale lemon glow in the west. When that faded, the night would come down like the drawing of a curtain. If his guards chose to desert him then, Stan would be lost.

He began to feel at the top of his right boot, as if it were giving him trouble, pausing a moment, then hurrying on to catch up with the two Lapps. He hoped to lull them into a sense of security, and then to make a bolt for it.

Stopping once more he bent and began to fiddle with the top of his boot. His Lapp guards slowed down, but after a cursory glance, did not bother to watch him.

Stan turned and ran for a large ice-hummock. If he could get a few yards start, he might shake off his guards. With darkness approaching he might get away and make his way back to the ship—though what would happen then he did not care to contemplate.

Crack!

The dark-faced Lapps, however, were on the alert, as the firing of the first shot proved. The bullet kicked up chips of ice a foot in front of Stan, then whined off into the gloom.

With the hummock only a few yards away, Stan dodged from side to side, praying that the next shot would miss. Another bullet kicked ice-chips on one side of him. Then he flung himself behind the hummock. As he scrambled behind the ice Stan heard the Lapps shouting, and it spurred him on. He scrambled through the mushy snow, slipping and sliding. Then he stopped. The Lapps must have guessed exactly what he would do, for while one followed him the other veered to the left and cut off his retreat.

The Lapp barred the way, gun held carelessly at hip level. Stan would have felt better if the man had been angry, but he stood there without the shadow of any feeling on his face. It was as if he had known something like this would happen, and had been prepared for it. The second Lapp arrived, and without a word the interrupted journey was resumed.

The only difference was that the Lapps now

walked a trifle quicker. They were among more broken ice, and walking was hard work. Stan's thighs began to ache. A ship's engine-room did not prepare a man for this kind of labour.

They passed evidence of the gruesome business of sealing—clustered seal carcases, ice stained with blood, empty cartridge cases.

Finally they halted. Before them was a lane of water some eight feet wide. The taller of the two Lapps indicated that Stan should jump the gap. Stan shook his head. His legs felt wooden, his feet a ton weight. He knew he could not possibly get across.

Again the Lapps motioned Stan to jump. Again he shook his head. Then the taller Lapp whipped his rifle round and hit the Britisher in the back with the butt. It was a brutal blow. Stan gasped, then wheeled and hit back.

His gloved fist took the Lapp full in the face. It was a satisfying blow, and struck square and solid. What was more, it threw the Lapp off balance. He went backwards with a tremendous splash into the icy water, his rifle vanishing with him.

Stan turned to the second guard; but his luck was out. The man lifted his gun and managed an awkward sideways swipe. Stan ducked; but the barrel took him across the temple.

The full force of the blow was deadened a little by the earflaps on his fur cap; but Stan went down, his eyes filled with a million flashing lights.

The Lapp jumped back, rifle ready, but Stan sprawled motionless. Gasping, and spitting water, the other Lapp scrambled on to the ice. He kicked Stan in the ribs, then started for the ship at a trot, followed by his friend.

Five or six minutes later Stan rolled on to his side, then slowly sat up. He lifted a hand to his temple, and winced. There was a lump on the side of his forehead which sent an excruciating pain through him when he fingered it. He sat for a few minutes then got shakily to his feet.

In the west a patch of lighter blue suggested where the sun had gone down, but overhead the stars were brightening. The daylight had gone for at least eighteen hours.

Painfully, Stan climbed a twelve-foot ice-hummock, and the exertion made his head swim. He rested for a few minutes and then scanned the horizon. It was a poor horizon, no farther than forty yards to the next shadowy masses of ice.

There were no lights to indicate either the *Bear*, or any other ship. If he had been the last man on earth he could not have felt more alone, or more forlorn at that moment.

Sliding down the hummock he laid a course by the stars, which he hoped would take him back to the *Bear*, and then began his painful journey.

Within a couple of minutes Lady Luck came to his aid. He saw the sheen of starlight at his feet, just as he was in the act of stepping into one of the numerous open lanes which dissected the ice-field. Another step and he would have been in the water.

He laughed, but it was a shaky laugh.

"You'd better sit down, my lad," he muttered. "This isn't your lucky day. Once it comes morning it shouldn't be too difficult to find your way back."

He was talking for talking's sake. Deep down inside him he knew he would never find his way back. Once Thorson collected his crew he would move off to begin robbing the sealing ships working in that neighbourhood.

"If I don't find Thorson," Stan consoled himself, "I'm sure to come across one of the sealers. They've been here." But that very thought damped his spirits. The sealers had already combed this district—the many skinned-carcases proved that—therefore they were unlikely to come back again.

After a minute or so he began to whistle, and even in the blackness of his position he had to smile, for the tune which came unbidden to his mind started:

"When you come to the end of a perfect day
    And sit alone with your thoughts."

Aboard the *Bear* there was jubilation. The Russian patrol vessel had been, and gone. She had hove-to a cable's length away, and a boarding party had searched the *Bear* very thoroughly. The ship's papers had been examined and returned, pronounced correct in every detail. The lack of sealskins Thorson got over by a story of engine trouble which had delayed them. They had only just begun sealing. The absence of most of the crew gave weight to this story, and the Russians were satisfied.

The Bofors gun, the dummy guns, the ammunition, and the steel protecting grilles for the bridge went undiscovered, all safely stored in an oil tank prepared specially for the purpose.

Thorson had played the part of an outraged captain, protesting vigorously against the illegal search; but he had been rewarded merely with a stiff salute and a wintry smile.

With a sullen crunching of ice beneath her massive bows the three-thousand tonner had moved off, to intercept another sealer, and the danger to the *Bear* was over.

Thorson was jubilant, but Jimmy Staton did not share his glee. He took Thorson into the stateroom and held out a slip of paper. It was the note Stan Farrager had left on the panel by the engine-room controls. Its message was brief, but very much to the point. It said:

"If you start the diesels without me to rectify them, there will be an explosion. S. Farrager."

"I found it in the engine-room when I went down with the search party," Staton said.

Thorson read and re-read the warning, while his face darkened and the veins on his temples stood out as his anger mounted. Finally he turned accusingly to Staton and roared:

"He must have been warned. I purposely pretended to be in a good humour to allay any suspicions he might have. There's somebody running with the hare *and* the hounds. And if I find out——" He did not finish his threat, but he stared at Staton accusingly.

Jimmy Staton laughed, a nasty, sarcastic laugh.

"Listen," he said curtly. "Farrager's no fool. Would you take precautions if you were in his shoes? I should. You're not the only one who looks ahead. I knew Farrager when I was a kid; he's smart. Smart enough to make sure you don't leave him on the ice."

"But I will," Thorson ranted. "He's bluffing. He wasn't down in the engine-room for more than a few minutes. He couldn't have done anything."

"He was down long enough for you to start bawling for him to hurry," Staton pointed out. "Anyway, I wouldn't do anything rash if I were you."

"I'll start the diesels now," Thorson snapped. "I'll soon call his bluff."

"Give me five minutes to pack a bit of food. I want to get on the ice before you do it," Staton said quietly. "I'm not staying here while you call Farrager's bluff. I know him. He won't risk his life on a bluff. If he says there'll be an explosion, there'll be one."

Thorson raged up and down. He cursed Staton

for a coward and a traitor. He cursed the two engine-room helpers for their ignorance of diesel engines, and generally behaved like a madman. One member of the crew who came to see what was wrong, was knocked down and kicked unconscious.

Through it all Staton remained calmly aloof, smoking a cigarette. Finally he went on to the bridge, and from the starboard wing looked out across the ice.

An hour later he went into the big stateroom. Thorson was chewing the end of an unlit cheroot, his eyes evil, his face a mask of devilish hate.

"The crew are aboard," Staton said quietly, "including the two Lapps who took Farrager out. You could send them back for him before it is too late."

Thorson remained silent, staring across the room. Finally he lit his cheroot. Smoking seemed to dissolve his evil temper for he suddenly rose and stalked out on deck.

The crew were called from their quarters where they were just starting the evening meal. They mustered in uneasy silence, conscious that something untoward had happened. Thorson called for the two Lapps who had disposed of Stan Farrager, and ordered them to bring the Britisher back to the ship.

"It is too dark," one of them protested, "and he may have started to look for some other ship."

Thorson knocked the man down. The Lapp got

to his feet, one hand to his bleeding mouth, and there was no more arguing.

In view of the possible difficulties Thorson ordered all hands out on the search, and ten minutes later a line of dancing lights across the ice showed where the unwilling crew were starting out. They were not to return without Farrager.

Thorson went down to the engine-room. Everything looked normal. The green covers of the diesels gave no hint of devilry within. The brasswork was gleaming. There was a warm comfortable smell of oil; it was a picture of a well-cared-for engine-room.

Twice Thorson decided to start the engines, and each time Jimmy Staton reminded him that the success of the whole business was threatened.

"It's being tricked by that swine which gets me," Thorson screeched. "When I see these engines are working again, Jimmee, I'll kill him. I'll kill him with my own hands!"

Jimmy Staton lit another cigarette and remained silent. When things went wrong Thorson was vicious enough for anything, and Staton was wondering what would happen if Stan Farrager was brought back alive.

Two hours later lights were seen in the distance, heralding the return of the search party. And Thorson went on deck to watch them come aboard. He was silent when Stan, wet and shivering, was helped over the rail. Unable to keep warm, and deciding anything was better than quietly freezing to death, the Britisher had started to walk. With-in five minutes he had gone through a thin crust of mush-ice, and was now soaked to the skin.

In the galley he stripped off his clothing and sitting before the roaring fire drank a cup of scalding coffee. Staton looked in, went away, and sent along a change of clothing.

By the time he had been aboard twenty minutes, Stan was feeling almost himself again. He had eaten a gargantuan meal, had swilled strong, sweet coffee, and his shivering had ceased.

Then Thorson sent for him.

Stan was escorted down to the engine-room. Two rather scared greasers were there. Staton was standing quietly by the control panel, and Thorson was by his side, chewing on an unlit cheroot.

"Ah, Mr. Farrager," Thorson's voice was suave, pleasant; the voice of a friend. "Glad to have you back again. I'm afraid my Lapps made a serious mistake in leaving you out there."

"Yes, I think they did," Stan agreed dryly, and in the same breath asked: "Perhaps you got a note I left for you. I don't see it about."

"Yes—we got it," Thorson said, still good-humoured, "of course we realised you were joking. Nevertheless, I did not have the diesels started until you came back. Anyway, perhaps you will start them now. I want to get away from here and be ready for business when daylight comes."

"I'm sorry," Stan was just as quiet, and just as

good-humoured as Thorson, "I meant every word on that slip of paper. You see, even if you brought *me* back—there is still Tubby Fenner."

"Tubby Fenner?" Thorson's eyebrows had gone up slightly, "I don't quite understand. What has he got to do with my engines? You are my engineer. I think that was understood when you gave me your promise, a promise with an Englishman's word of honour to back it up. You promised to obey my orders. I want you to start the engines."

"Not until Tubby Fenner is back on this ship," Stan told him. "If *you* want to start them—go ahead; but if you'll take my advice, you won't do anything until I've had a few minutes, alone, with the engines."

"You refuse to start them?" There was an edge to Thorson's voice.

"I do."

CHAPTER TEN

THORSON PLAYS THE "JOKER"

FOR a few moments there was silence in that spotless engine-room. The two greasers, though they understood not a word of English, realised something vital was happening. They could see the anger mounting in Thorson's face. They could tell the young Britisher was defiant . . . even if his face was pale. Jimmy Staton puffed at his cigarette—like a schoolboy trying his first forbidden smoke.

"If you refuse to obey orders, Mr. Farrager, you are no longer any use to me." As Thorson said that his right hand came out of his coat pocket, and it held an automatic pistol.

"Don't do anything rash," Jimmy Staton cautioned.

"I don't do rash things," Thorson said, his eyes holding Stan's, "I think first. Now, Farrager, choose. Start those diesels, or—take this," and he tapped the automatic with the forefinger of his left hand.

"You've asked for it," Stan said, and his nerves were so taut that the words were little more than a whisper. Once before he had called the bluff

of a man with a gun. Jimmy Staton had threatened him in the wireless cabin, but he had known
Jimmy Staton. He had felt instinctively that
Jimmy would not shoot him. With Thorson it
was different. This tall, dark-faced man had a
streak of madness in him somewhere. It showed
in his eyes, in the nervous twitchings of his face
muscles. Defiance infuriated him. Thorson could
be a killer.

"I've warned you," Stan whispered, and moved
across to the starting mechanism.

"And I've warned you," Thorson sneered. "You
thought you held the ace card, Mr. Farrager. You
thought I couldn't manage without an engineer.
I can, now. The visit of the Russian patrol ship
has put me in the clear. They won't touch me
again. They've decided the *Bear* is just another
sealer. That means I don't need my engines at
concert pitch all the time. I can manage, now,
with any fool who can stop and start the engines.
And now——"

"And so you think you can ditch me, eh?"
Thorson's gloating did something to Stan. The
queer fluttering in his throat was quietened by
rising anger. "All right. I'll start the engines,
Mr. Thorson. I don't want to die, but if I must,
I'll take you along with me."

"Stop wasting time."

Stan laid a hand on the high pressure air
control. Half a revolution would start the diesels
turning, the air pressure working in the same

way that a self-starter turns a motor car engine until it fires.

"If I go to hell, Mr. Thorson, you'll be with me." As he spoke, Stan gave the wheel a quarter turn.

For a moment nothing happened. Stan had only allowed the air valve to open a little, and it was taking rather longer than usual for the compressed air to start the diesels moving.

A further quarter turn, and there was a sudden low grumble. The diesels were starting to turn over. Almost at once there was an ominous grinding, slow, frightening, like the clashing of a gearbox of giant proportions.

"Stop it!" Jimmy Staton's nerve was not equal to the strain. He flung himself across and with a vicious jerk shut off the compressed air.

The awful clashing ceased.

Face bedewed with sweat, Staton turned to Thorson, and there was a note of hysteria in his voice when he screamed:

"You mad fool. Do you want to ruin everything If the diesels are damaged we're finished. I'm risking as much as you and I'm having the rewards. Do you hear me, you lunatic?"

Stan leaned against the starter, and waited. He felt weak and shaken. He was playing the biggest game of bluff any man could play. There was no risk of an explosion. The most that could happen, if the diesels were started, would be the stripping of some teeth from the helical gearing. Stan had set the gears not quite in reverse, so that they were grinding viciously. If there had been any one there with a real knowledge of engines, his bluff would have been called at once.

His bluff had almost been called. Thorson would have gone through with it, but Jimmy Staton's nerves had not been equal to the strain.

What was passing through Thorson's mind no one could guess. Suddenly he turned on his heel and made for the deck. Just as he was climbing out of sight he called down:

"All right, Farrager. Come up!"

Stan blew out a gusty sigh of relief. Jimmy Staton, however, was still sweating, and he whispered a warning:

"Don't drive him too far, Stan. You don't know how dangerous he is. Be reasonable, I tell you, he's a killer."

"Thanks," Stan looked at his one-time friend, then said soberly: "He's killing Tubby Fenner at this minute, Jimmy. Why don't *you* do something? You know what it's like on the ice. Tubby's freezing to death out there. For God's sake, Jimmy, be a man, if it's only for to-night. Send someone out for Tubby Fenner."

"I'm not the boss here," Staton growled, and refused to meet Stan's gaze. "Short of killing Thorson I can't do anything for Fenner."

Stan followed him on deck wondering what the next phase in the drama would be. He was not left long in doubt. The moment Stan stepped out on deck he was grabbed by three men and, struggle though he did, his clothes were torn off him. Left only with a torn vest and a pair of trunks, he was held against the rail, shivering in the bitter cold.

Five minutes went by, and Stan was trembling from head to foot, his teeth chattering uncontrollably. The cold was biting deeper every second. Ten minutes of this would reduce him to unconsciousness.

He was, in fact, only half conscious when Thorson ordered him to be taken to the galley. The galley fire was roaring. The smell of freshly brewed coffee made the air aromatic.

"Give him a drink," Thorson snapped, and watched while one man held Stan's lower jaw to prevent his chattering teeth from chipping the cup. They poured strong, scaldingly hot coffee into him. They wrapped him in hot blankets, and Stan slowly came back to normality. He looked at Thorson, and thought he knew what was in his devilish mind.

Thorson was in no hurry. He went on deck for a few minutes, and coming back took off his thick gloves and warmed his hands at the galley fire.

"It's very comfortable in here, Mr. Farrager," he said quietly. "It's cold on deck . . . even for a man who is fully dressed. I don't want to have to put you out again, naked."

Stan was pale. The ordeal through which he had passed would remain vivid to his dying day, and he did not want a repetition of it. He knew what Thorson would do. The man intended to expose Stan to the cold again and again until his prisoner weakened, and finally admitted defeat. It was fiendish cruelty, but it could gain Thorson a victory.

"There isn't any need for you to suffer," Thorson went on soothingly, "but you are holding a pistol at my head and I don't let any man do that."

"I didn't ask to come with you," Stan told him.

"You were a necessity," Thorson snapped, and then, as if remembering he must keep calm, he went on smoothly: "Mr. Farrager, be reasonable and there need be no more trouble. Work with me and I'll see you are handsomely paid when the trip is over. I'll put you ashore at some convenient place in Britain. I'll supply you with an alibi to prove you did not willingly desert your ship. Now, can I do more?"

"You can send a party out to look for Tubby Fenner."

Thorson stared silently at Stan, then shook his head, and his silence was more ominous than his previous outbursts of maniacal rage.

"I'll give you a last chance," he said finally. "Tell me what you have done to the diesels. Or you can swim for it."

"You know my terms." Stan was surprised at the firmness of his voice. He knew Thorson was not bluffing, and he was afraid of what lay ahead.

Without answering Thorson left the galley.

"I wish I could do somethin' for ye," old Ben muttered, "but I can't."

A minute passed, during which time Thorson and Staton could be heard on deck arguing. Staton coldly logical, Thorson as coldly unbending.

The argument ceased. Two Finns came into the galley and motioned Stan to follow them. He drew the blankets about him but the Finns stripped him to his vest and shorts. Then he was hurried out on deck. The decklights were burning, now, and they cast a cold gleam on the mush-ice, and the lane of water in which the *Bear* was hove-to.

"Have you changed your mind?" Thorson asked.

"You've finished with your diesels, if you ditch me," Stan said, his teeth already chattering.

The next moment Stan was struggling in the grip of four men. They swept him off his feet, swung him back, forward, back again, then threw him up and out.

He tried to catch at the rail, missed it, had a momentary glimpse of black-looking water beneath . . . then went down and under with a splash which threw spray over the ship's rail.

There was an audible intake of breath from the watchers. The crew were a hard-bitten lot, but this deliberate murder was something which shocked even them.

"Now," Thorson said, turning away. "Get the

others out. . . . I'll have that fat engineer brought in. I've stood——"

A moment later he reeled backwards. Jimmy Staton had ripped into him with a terrific punch to the jaw, following it up with a left hook to the ribs. Thorson went down, and stayed down, while Jimmy stood over him, murder in his eyes. Thorson did not move. The first punch had been a knock-out.

"Get Farrager out!" Jimmy Staton had gone berserk, and when the nearest man just gaped at him, he was smacked against the rails with a swinging body punch which doubled him up, gasping.

There was a hurried scattering. Two men leapt on to the rail, poised there for a moment, then jumped for the fringe of the nearest ice. A moment later the deck lights showed for a second on the pale body of Stan Farrager as he came slowly to the surface. He was not moving, and began to sink again.

They got him on deck, and for the third time that night he was wrapped in hot blankets and massaged with work-roughened hands.

Jimmy Staton called the crew. Thorson stood on one side, one hand nursing his bruised jaw. He made no effort to intervene when Staton ordered all hands to search for Tubby Fenner. When the men had gone he turned and walked quietly to the stateroom.

When Staton had seen Stan Farrager restored

to consciousness, and put to bed, he went to the stateroom. Thorson was staring moodily across the room, an empty glass in his right hand, an unlit cheroot clasped in his left fist.

"Well," Staton said brusquely. "The next move is yours, Thorson. I'm not fool enough to believe I could get the crew to follow me. You're their boss."

Thorson was silent for a moment or so, but his left hand mangled the cheroot, until it was only a handful of shredded tobacco leaf. Finally he stood up and smiled.

"Jimmee—I think I picked better than I knew when I took you as a partner. That young Britisher had me on the brink of murder for days. He is too cool, too cunning. He's had the whip-hand. I had to get rid of him, or go mad!"

"You haven't got rid of him, y'know," Staton said crisply. "I dosed him with rum and he's asleep in his cabin now. I've sent for Tubby Fenner, too."

"I know. I ought to have agreed to it from the first . . . but I get a devil in me, Jimmee." For a moment it seemed as if his ill-temper would return but he conquered the impulse, and forced a smile. "There's one thing, Jimmee—we've got to get rid of both these Britishers."

Staton said nothing. Thorson produced his case and took out the last cheroot. He lit it, before saying:

"Jimmee, we've got to let these two men escape."

"Escape?" For a moment Staton wondered if his ears were tricking him.

"They won't agree to anything I suggest," Thorson went on. We can't take them back with us—they'd talk. You know what that would mean."

Staton nodded.

"If they got away in one of our boats," Thorson said quietly, "and if there was a storm blowing up about which they knew nothing, they wouldn't trouble us again. See what I mean, Jimmee? Let them escape, but make sure they don't have a cat in hell's chance."

"They wouldn't bite." Staton shook his head. "You will insist on thinking they're a couple of born fools. They're not. I don't know the fat man, but Stan Farrager's kept a jump ahead of you all the time. Do you think he wouldn't suspect a trick if he found everything laid on for a nice easy getaway? You'll have to think again."

Thorson chuckled, and puffed two perfect smoke rings. Then he looked across at Staton.

"Jimmee . . . you and this Farrager were friends, once. I suggest you suddenly repent. You have been a bad man; now you are sorry. Would it be too difficult? After all, you did save his life. And it did mean punching me—your partner." Thorson tenderly stroked his swollen jaw.

"I'm sorry about that," Staton said, "but I couldn't stomach cold-blooded murder."

"Of course you can't," Thorson agreed, and chuckled again, "that is why my plan will work. You are filled with remorse. Find an opportunity to talk to Farrager. Tell him that I mean to kill him. Therefore, for old times' sake, you have decided to help him and Fenner to escape."

Staton frowned, and Thorson continued:

"Offer to collect some stores for them, and help them get a boat out when the time is ripe. *I* shall choose the night of the escape." Thorson spoke with deliberate emphasis.

"No!" Staton said angrily. "It's murder."

"They *are* going to escape," Thorson insisted. "We made a mistake when we shanghaied them at Tromso. Suppose we took them back. Would they keep quiet?"

He shook his head as Jimmy Staton said nothing.

"In no time at all," Thorson went on, "the police of half the world would be looking for us. Jimmee, I have a great respect for the police. Once they know a man's identity, it is only a matter of time before they lay their hands on him. Can you imagine the headlines in your own country? 'One of the men behind the series of robberies from the sealing ships was a Britisher, none other than Jimmee Staton.'"

Staton sat down, his face troubled. Thorson could see he was winning.

"When we have finished, Jimmee, we'll be

wealthy. You will be able to live like a gentle-man."

"With two murders on my conscience?" Jimmy snapped.

"Will it be your fault if a storm catches them out in a small boat?" Thorson asked. "Come, Jimmee, be sensible."

Jimmy Staton stared across the table with eyes which were looking into the past. He and Stan Farrager had been boys together. They had enjoyed life, camping, tramping, climbing. Life had been good.

"It's them or you," Thorson broke in on his thoughts. "They've got to be silenced."

Staton groaned.

"Surely we could fix them some other way."

"No," Thorson said with finality. "It's them or us. Anyway, we'll give them a few days to get used to the idea that you are reformed, then, at the first promise of a really bad storm, *you* will help them to escape."

"Okay!" Jimmy rose and walked slowly out of the stateroom.

CHAPTER ELEVEN

PIRACY!

PALE LEMON sunbeams, slanting through the porthole, roused Stan Farrager from his heavy sleep. For a minute or so he lay quietly enjoying the half-awake, half-asleep state. Then, remembering where he was, he half-turned over and realised the old cook was in the cabin, staring at him.

"Awake, eh?" Ben rose from his chair, and nodded to show his satisfaction. "I'll get ye some breakfas', though it ain't so far off noon."

"Here, wait," Stan struggled to a sitting position, wincing as he did so. His body ached as if he had been pummelled for hours, and he felt as stiff as a board.

"Now, now, take it easy," Ben coaxed. "Time to talk later. I'll just get ye some coffee an' toast."

Stan was glad to lie back. His head throbbed savagely, and he felt both weak and depressed. He was trying to think what had happened when the gentle vibrating of the bunk told him the ship was under way.

Under way! It meant Thorson had discovered what was wrong with the diesels. That brought everything else back with a rush, and Stan shivered as he remembered the agonies of the previous night. The horror of standing almost naked in the freezing night air. Thorson's callousness, and the awful moment when he was thrown overboard. What had happened afterwards he could not remember. When he hit the water something seemed to burst in his head. There had been a great flash of light . . . then darkness.

He was still pondering when Ben came back, bringing a tray. The aroma of the coffee made Stan realise how desperately hungry he was. He had eaten only once since midday the previous day and there had been that ghastly tramp across the ice before the search party had rescued him, just in time.

"This here toast ought to be hard as iron." Old Ben broke in on his thoughts, and chuckled as he poured coffee, while he held out a piece of toast which dripped butter. "It's been done nigh on two hours . . . but I reckoned it'd be right enough, chance I put enough butter on it. How're you feelin', Mister?"

"Not too bad," Stan admitted, ignoring the toast and waiting for the coffee. "What happened? Who started the diesels? Where are we now?"

"Now, one at a time, one at a time," Ben protested, handing up the creamy coffee. "First of all—your pal's aboard again. In the engine-room at this very minute. An'——"

"Tubby aboard!" Stan almost upset his coffee at the news, and in his relief he could have leapt out of the bunk. "How is he?"

"His sort never takes no harm," Ben retorted, and winked. "If he fell off a church, he'd let on a passin' haycart! Nothin' ever goes wrong with his kind. I've seen 'em before."

"Did he come back by himself?"

"No." Ben shook his head, tiptoed to the cabin door, looked out, then hurried back. In a whisper he said, "Mr. Staton rescued you. He hit Cap'n Thorson! Cor, what a smasher it were, too. Knocked him for six just as you splashed into the drink. Then he orders the crew to go after Tubby—that were after we'd got you out."

"Jimmy Staton!" Stan was incredulous.

"Aye, it were him right enough," Ben agreed. "What went on 'tween him and Cap'n Thorson afterwards, I don't know; they seem friendly enough this mornin'. The crew brought Mr. Fenner back just before dawn . . . an' there were nothin' wrong with him."

"After so long?"

"His sort are born lucky," Ben insisted. "Found some sealskins an' wrapped hisself in 'em. He stunk awful when he come aboard, but there was nothin' wrong with him."

"Did he start the engines?" Stan asked, anxious to know who had repaired that bit of work.

"I dunno," Ben was obviously unaware of the bogus sabotage. "We didn't start movin' till daylight came, Mr. Fenner went below, like he were makin' for the engine-room."

"Hm!" Stan drank deep of the delicious coffee, then took one of the pieces of toast, soggy with butter, and toasted a golden colour.

"There's one thing," Ben said, after a short pause, "Cap'n Thorson seems in a rare good humour again, an' that's somethin' to be thankful for. He's a devil when he's in a bad temper."

"Does he know I'm awake?"

"Not him. An' I don't reckon he'll be interested for an hour or so," Ben chuckled. "We're headin' for a sealer. We'll be startin' the good work any minute."

"The *good* work?" Stan queried.

Ben grunted non-committally.

"Well, we all gets a share o' the proceeds," he said, "and if we don't make a sizeable wage packet—an' us not having to hunt for seals, I don't reckon we ever will. There's forty aboard, and we all gets threepence in every quid that's taken."

"Threepence! Well, forty threepences only make ten shillings," Stan pointed out, "Who gets . . ."

"Cap'n and Mr. Staton has to have their whack," Ben said, "and there's expenses. We've only borrowed this craft. I reckons the owner'll have a pink fit if ever he finds out what his ship's been a-doing of. Lor . . . it makes me laugh to think of it. Thorson chartered the *Bear* off an Italian Count. Millionaire once, but so danged poor now he nearly fell over hisself when Thorson offers to charter the ship for three months."

"Thorson must have laid out a packet of money: food, fuel and so on." Stan wanted to get to know as much as possible about the business, but old Ben suddenly realised he was talking too glibly, and he shut up like a clam.

"I'd better get the dinner goin'," he muttered, and went out.

About one o'clock Stan was conscious of a change in the ship's speed. The *Bear* vibrated as her twin screws went into reverse, threshing the icy water into foam. Finally the vibrations ceased, and the ship was still.

From the porthole Stan could see nothing but ice; but he still felt too shaky to go on deck, nor did he want to draw attention to the fact that he was awake. Apparently only the cook knew of that for the moment. Listening intently he heard the voice of someone shouting through megaphones. Then the shouting stopped, and all was silent.

If Tubby had not come to the cabin to enlighten him as to what was going on, Stan might have ventured up above to see for himself. The sound of footsteps, however, sent him scuttling to his bunk, and when the burly Geordie entered the cabin, Stan was lying beneath the blankets, his eyes closed, his breathing as steady as that of a babe.

"Ah, he's had some breakfast," Tubby noted the

tray, the empty coffee jug and the crumbs of toast. "That's a——"

"Tubby!" Stan sat up so quickly he made his friend start back in surprise. "What's going on outside?"

"Eh, man, but it's good to see you alive again," Tubby grabbed Stan's hands, and wrung them thankfully. "Lor, but I've been sweatin' blood for ye. When I saw you earlier I wouldn't have given tuppence for you. Breathing heavy as a grampus, you was, and your face as pale as wax. I didn't know, then, what they'd been doing to you. Old Ben told me afterwards. Cor, if I get the chance, I'll screw Thorson's neck round till it comes right off his shoulders, the murdering swine."

"Oh, forget it!" Stan laughed sheepishly.

"Forget it!" Tubby snorted. "Ben told me what you did. Man, you were wonderful. But for you I'd still be out on the ice, and——"

"For the second time—forget it!" Stan felt happier than for a long time. "You'd have done the same for me. Tell me, who started the diesels?"

Tubby leaned back and laughed.

"You're smart, Stan. When I tumbled to what you'd done—bluffed that rat into rescuing me—and all with nothing more than a gear quarter-engaged, I could have laughed in his face. I couldn't have thought of anything like that. They still don't know what you did. I chucked everybody out of the engine-room while I put the thing right. Thorson still thinks there was something terrific brewing."

"What are we stopped for?"

Tubby's smile faded.

"He's on with his programme."

"Robbing a sealer?"

Tubby nodded.

"Yes, he's got his Bofors gun rigged up again. The crew are dressed in Russian naval uniform, with Thorson in yards of gold braid. We're flying the Soviet flag, and when I left the deck they were getting ready to bring over the first batch of sealskins."

"There's going to be a terrible row over this," Stan prophesied.

Tubby nodded soberly, then said:

"Staton spoke to me. I don't trust him, but I think he's got the wind up."

"Oh, why?"

"He got me by myself," Tubby explained, "and said: 'If I offered you a chance to get away, what would you say?'"

"Jimmy said that?" Stan was suddenly excited. "Y'know, Tubby, he was my best pal years ago. In those days you could have staked your life on him."

"I wouldn't stake a bad penny on him," Tubby jeered. "I know what's wrong with him, Stan. He's scared, and he wants to have a foot in both camps. He wants to have somebody who'll speak up for him when they're caught."

"What did you say to him?" Stan asked eagerly.

"I just looked him up and down," Tubby chuckled, "then I shook my head. 'Pull the other leg, matey,' I said, and walked away."

Stan shook his head: "You're hopeless, Tubby, you could have——"

"Don't get het-up," Tubby broke in. "I know which side my bread's buttered, man. And I know what'll happen if we don't get away from here quick—but it doesn't pay to lap up the first bit o' cream that's offered. If Staton's keen to help us, thinks I, he'll come again."

"That's what you think."

"Yes, an' I were right," Tubby said ponderously, "Matey, our old Vicar back home used to tell my mother: 'That boy's as cunning as a barrel o' monkeys, and he's got a tongue that could get him out of any fix.' And the Vicar knew me; I were one of his choir boys for four years. Anyway, Staton did come again. He slipped me a paper. Want to read it?" He grinned and held the paper out of reach as Stan leaned forward to take it.

"Don't be a fool!" Stan was not in the mood for joking, and Tubby gave him the paper.

"It don't say much," Tubby said, "but it's a sign o' the times. Your pal's seen the red light. I suppose he thinks if he helps us it's something in his favour later on."

Stan did not reply. He read and re-read the note. It was short and to the point:

"T. means to get rid of you. I'll see what I
can do. I will try and see you for a minute,
later. Jaton."

"Must have been in a desperate hurry when he
signed it," Tubby suggested. "When a fellow can't
spell his own name it looks like——"

"That's not a mistake," Stan said. "That was a
signature he used when we were kids. I used to
sign my notes 'Stafar,' first syllable of my
Christian and surnames."

"Oh," Tubby sounded almost disappointed to
discover that Staton had deliberately signed his
note "Jaton."

"Anyway, it proves one thing," Stan said
jubilantly. "Jimmy wouldn't have signed his note
that way, if it wasn't to remind me that we had
been pals."

"I don't trust him," Tubby said dourly. "I'll
take all the help he offers, but everything'll have
to be shipshape and Bristol fashion, no monkey
tricks. He'd double-cross us as soon as spit out."

Stan refused to argue, and the burly Geordie
went off to the engine-room, while Stan lay back
to recover his strength.

Later in the day he went on deck, as the last
batch of skins was being transferred from the
sealer to the *Bear*. Thorson was jubilant. They
had got well over a thousand sculps, and his eyes
were on another sealer which was slowly working
her way nearer.

Later, before they robbed the second sealer, Stan got a close-up of what sealing was like, and it gave him some idea of the amazing physique of the men who went across the mush-ice hunting seals.

In the crow's nest of the sealer a man was conning the ship through the mush-ice. Over an area of at least a square mile the intermittent crack of rifles had been going on steadily for hours, and there were bloodied patches of snow and ice everywhere. Men were laboriously dragging three or four sealskins to the ship, others hurrying out again after more. When the gunners had slaughtered one batch of seals they hurried on, a boy at their heels carrying ammunition. The skinners separated skin from carcase with long, deft strokes of the knife. Then a leather thong was threaded through the eyeholes. When he had three or four skins the skinner would turn for the ship . . . leaning forward the better to haul his load across the mush-ice.

The parent ship never stopped, and it seemed a miracle that some of her crew were not left behind. Several seemed at their last gasp when they were hauled aboard, yet a few minutes later they would be leaping out again on to the ice, spurred on by the vitriolic tongue of their captain in the crow's nest.

"They gets two meals a day." It was Ben who had joined Stan for a moment. "It's a hell of a life . . . an' that's why every man aboard this ship is ready to take a chance on hi-jacking. Ordinary sealin' lasts a couple o' months; eighteen, and sometimes twenty hours a day . . . eat, sleep, eat . . . then work till you drops. Often you're wet to the thighs . . . but you gets no chance o' changing. If you are really done up when you gets back, the cap'n mebbe will let 'em have a mouthful of coffee. Then you're off again. There's no let-up when you're sealin'. As long as there's light to see for shootin' and skinnin' . . . well, you shoots and you skins."

The sealer captain went on working until dusk had deepened into night. Then Thorson rang down for half-speed, and the *Bear* came to life again. She moved in for her second "boarding" of the day. Menaced by the Bofors gun, and by a dozen smartly clad sailors, the exhausted crew of the sealer were forced to allow the *Bear* to come alongside. The night was refreshingly calm, and all through the early hours of darkness work went on, while the crew of the sealer made the air sulphurous with their complaints, as they helped transfer their catch.

When the last skin had been taken aboard the *Bear*, Thorson, with ironic politeness, handed to the captain of the sealer a note, signed on behalf of the Soviet Union, acknowledging receipt of 1,326 sealskins.

It was when they were moving off that Jimmy Staton contacted Stan, and he seemed very nervous.

"You'd see the note I gave Fenner," he began.

"Thorson means to get rid of you both. If I can get you some food, would you risk getting away in a boat?"

"Are you coming with us?"

Staton shook his head.

"Daren't. There's too much against me. No, but I'll help you. It'll have to be at night—so hold yourself ready each evening. I'll try and make it between seven and nine. I sometimes relieve the deck watch. Are you game?"

"Yes, and thanks a lot."

"You'll have to take your chance of getting aboard one of the sealing ships," Staton went on, "but at least it's a sporting chance. Tell Fenner not to look so pleased with himself. Thorson might get suspicious."

With that he hurried away.

For the next three days the weather remained reasonably calm, and Thorson "made hay while the sun shone." He steamed hard from ship to ship, always making sure that when he boarded a vessel there was no other in the vicinity. In forty-eight hours he robbed six ships, and each time he arranged for the victim's wireless to be "accidentally" put out of action.

The evening of the third day Thorson listened to the weather report going out to shipping from the big station on Greenland, as well as from Brest. From North Cape to Kara Straits, which included the White Sea area, there was going to be a severe "blow." Coming straight from the north, it would bring snow and sleet squalls. The Arctic Winter was preparing a last bad-tempered attack before the approaching spring brought more warmth from the sun, and longer days.

Armed with news of the approaching storm, Thorson sought out Jimmy Staton. He could not keep the jubilation out of his voice.

"Jimmee . . you can play the Good Samaritan this very night. Help our two British guests to escape. Let them take the starboard boat. You needn't overload it with supplies. I don't see the point of wasting good food. They'll never eat it."

"You're determined on this?" Staton asked.

"You know it's the only way," Thorson snapped, and Jimmy nodded.

"Okay, I'll go and tell them."

CHAPTER TWELVE

TUBBY IS TOO SUSPICIOUS

THE *Bear* always hove-to at night, and Tubby was with Stan in the cabin when Staton slipped in to see them.

"I've fixed things," he announced. "Food, spare clothing, and if I can find a spare compass, I will. We are not too far from the tip of the Kanin Peninsula. Get there and signal one of the sealers. Then you are safe."

"Unless you came along to pinch the catch," Tubby pointed out, "then we'd be in the soup worse than ever."

Staton shrugged.

"That's a chance you'll have to take," he admitted, "I can't guarantee anything; you know that. If you were caught again, I'd expect you to keep mum about my part in your escape."

"Why don't you come with us," Stan pleaded. "Come on, Jimmy. Drop this stupid racket. If we get away we could cook up some yarn which would put you in the clear."

Staton shook his head.

"No, Stan. I told you before—I'm not the reforming kind. I've had a tough deal, and I'm out for easy money."

"You're going to be disappointed," Tubby prophesied. "You'll start an international row that'll blow the United Nations to bits. Russian pride won't——"

"Oh, stow that," Staton snapped, and turning to the door paused just long enough to add: "Don't move out of here till I come for you. I'll get Thorson drinking to keep him off the deck." With that he left them.

He hurried back to Thorson and reported that everything was fixed. Thorson nodded and smiled.

"All right, Jimmee. You collect some food, and I'll make the other arrangements."

"What other arrangements?"

Thorson shook his head, and smiled.

"That's my business, Jimmee. Go on—we don't want this storm to blow up before they get away."

Staton went out. He looked worried as he collected food and spare clothing. The former he chose with care. Despite Thorson's suggestion that he need not pack much food, Staton filled two boxes. He packed a lot of sardines done in oil, chocolate, matches, some candles. Into the boxes went biscuits, bully beef and, equally important, two tin-openers.

While he was busy, Thorson was also hard at work. With a carpenter's brace and a one-inch boring bit he climbed on to the boat deck, and busied himself with the starboard boat.

Despite the chill night air he perspired freely

before he was through, for he bored twenty one-inch diameter holes in the bottom boards of the boat, and carefully caulked each hole with a loosely rolled plug of newspaper.

He estimated that within an hour the normal softening effect of water, plus the friction of the minute particles of ice along the keel of the boat would wash out the plugs. Twenty holes could not possibly be replugged. Even if the boat did not sink, the storm which was due in an hour or so would put a swift end to Tubby and Stan. Arctic storms were bitter. They threatened even well-kept ships. For men caught out on the open ice, there was only one end, and it was the end Thorson desired.

At five minutes past seven Thorson was back in the stateroom, smoking and sipping a glass of whisky. He was there when Jimmy Staton arrived to say that everything was ready; the food and clothing packed.

"Still going through with it?" he asked, and Thorson nodded.

"I am."

Staton sighed.

"All right, I'll get going. I've fixed the watch deck. I don't know how long it will take us to swing the boat off her davits."

"You are slipping, Jimmee," Thorson pointed out. "You forget I had all the boats swung out to-day, the falls checked, the blocks freshly greased. Come back when you are through . . . and we'll have a drink to celebrate."

"Okay."

"Oh," Thorson checked Staton at the door. "Don't forget, it's the starboard boat they take. Make sure of that."

Jimmy Staton nodded, and went on deck.

When he entered the cabin where Stan and Tubby were waiting he interrupted a lively discussion. Tubby Fenner was growing more and more suspicious.

"There's one thing you can't overlook," Tubby had been saying. "If we get away safely, the fat will be in the fire immediately. Even Staton isn't fool enough to think we'd keep quiet. In no time there'd be half a dozen gunboats racing for the Murmansk coast, guns out for the *Bear*. No, Stan, there's something fishy about this escape racket."

"I know it looks suspicious," Stan had replied, "but Jimmy Staton was a pal of mine. He wouldn't double-cross me."

Tubby gave a sarcastic grunt.

"There are black sheep in every family, my lad. Staton may have been a good sort once, but he's gone off the rails. He's a bad egg, and bad eggs stink. This ' escape offer ' stinks."

It was at this juncture Jimmy Staton entered. He nodded to them but wasted no time in useless talk.

"We've got about an hour," he announced.

"I've packed a couple of boxes with grub and spare clothes. There are matches and candles, as well; I couldn't find a compass, but you should be able to steer by the stars. We're dead north of Kanin at this moment. You should see the headland when daylight breaks."

They followed him on deck. There was an unusual hush about the air. Normally, at this time, a thin wind was keening over the ship, making the ice-shrouded rigging sing and whine plaintively. The silence, now, was ominous. Overhead, the sky was blackening with piling cumulus, and through the breaks to the north it was just possible to see wheeling spokes of light, a display from Aurora Borealis . . . always an indication of worsening weather. Apart from the riding lights, the ship was in darkness.

"Here are the two boxes," Jimmy Staton had led them across to the port side, and he indicated two boxes, hidden against the rail. "I've oiled the blocks of the port boat, so she'll move out without too much row."

"I fancy the starboard boat," Tubby said, bending to lift one of the boxes. "I like the looks of it. Is there any reason why we shouldn't have that one?"

"None, except that I've oiled the blocks of the port boat," Staton snapped, and went on: "Look, I'm taking a big risk for you. I've got the port boat ready . . . and you'll go in the port boat, or not at all."

"Oh, well, if that's how you feel," Tubby said resignedly, and hefted the box under his left arm, then, without warning, he swung a right-hand punch. It was a perfect knock-out blow from the start. It took Jimmy Staton just below the ear, and he dropped without even a gasp.

Stan Farrager gaped. It was entirely unexpected and for the moment he was petrified, thinking they had been discovered; but the darkened ship was still quiet. No one moved. There was not the least hint of a suspicious sound.

"What . . . what's the idea?" he demanded. "What did you do that for, you fool?"

"For the moment, Stan, I'm taking charge," Tubby said grimly. "Your Jimmy may have been a good pal, once, but I don't trust him, and that's that."

"But he——"

"Listen to me," Tubby butted in. "If he was on the level he wouldn't care a tinker's curse which boat we took, and that gaff about oiling the blocks of this port boat specially for to-night is all my eye and Betty Martin. This afternoon the crew swung *all* boats, and oiled *all* davits. See what I mean?"

"He's coming round," Stan whispered, still feeling too bewildered to argue.

"In that case we'll do what they did to us when they knocked us out in Tromso," Tubby said feelingly. "He'll know what being gagged means, before I've finished with him."

Stan merely nodded. Tubby's unexpected action had robbed him of all initiative.

Jimmy Staton was gagged and bound and when he began to struggle Tubby lifted him and balanced him on the rail.

"I don't like you, my lad," the burly "Geordie" said darkly, "and any excuse to drop you over the rail will be good enough for me. Keep quiet, or over you go."

Staton ceased wriggling, and while Stan and Tubby climbed up to the starboard boat, he tried to chew through the gag which silenced him. It was hopeless. Tubby had had no sympathy with him and he had tied that gag tightly and securely.

Tubby and Stan struggled with the starboard boat, blissfully unaware that it had been tampered with. Tubby was triumphant as the davits swung round without the semblance of a squeak.

"What did I tell you?" he demanded. "Him and his port boat . . . davits oiled so they won't make any noise. He's a dirty double-crosser, Stan. I can smell 'em, and he stinks worse than any I've ever met."

Stan said nothing.

Putting their boxes into the boat they unbent the falls, and lowered the boat. It struck the water with a slap, despite the purchase offered by the double-sheaved blocks.

They listened but the ship was still silent, so silent they could hear the faint hum of the lighting set, and accordion music from the fo'csle.

"Now, my lad, down you go. I'll follow," Tubby ordered, but Stan shook his head.

"What's wrong?" Tubby was impatient.

"Look, Tubby, I hate leaving Staton."

"What?" Tubby Fenner was incredulous. "Don't be a fool, man. He wouldn't thank you for taking him away from the *Bear*. And the moment he was free he'd do his best to put a spoke in our wheel. I know his type, Stan, he's dangerous."

"Tubby! I knew Jimmy Staton years ago," Stan said firmly. "I don't care what he is, I'm not going to leave him here. Let's give him another chance! If he did try any funny business, we're two to one. What do you say?"

Tubby Fenner grunted.

"My experience with lame dogs, Stan, is they'll bite your fingers the moment you hold out a biscuit to 'em. You're crazy . . . but if you insist . . . okay."

"I'll not forget this," Stan whispered, but Tubby only grunted sarcastically.

Tiptoeing to the port side, they picked up Jimmy Staton and carried him to where the starboard boat was bobbing uneasily in the water.

Staton began to struggle the moment he was in the boat. He wanted to warn them against pushing off in this starboard boat. What Thorson had done to it he had no idea, but he was certain Thorson had done something and with a storm blowing up they would not have a chance of surviving.

Tubby pushed off, and masses of ice chips grated against the planking. When they were well clear of the *Bear*, the two Britishers began to row lustily. If they only got a few hundred yards away, before their absence was discovered, they would have at least a sporting chance. The food and extra clothing Staton had provided would keep then going for some time.

Jimmy Staton struggled desperately with his bonds, but he made no progress, and when they had been moving about ten minutes, following the lane of open water in which the *Bear* had been hove-to, Staton had a sudden shock. Water was seeping over the bottom boards. It was icy, and made him shiver. At least one of the paper plugs had worked loose from the holes Thorson had bored in the planking.

Staton struggled even more furiously, but for a few moments neither Tubby nor Stan took the slightest notice. They were putting all they knew into the rowing, for a wind was getting up. It came in gentle puffs; puffs which carried a dank chill, presaging the storm of which the radio had warned a few hours earlier.

"Lie still, you worm," Tubby Fenner looked over his shoulder, and then cursed as Staton, by a supreme effort, lifted his feet and crashed them on to the seat by Tubby's side.

Tubby swept Staton's booted feet off the seat,

then stiffened. There had been a distinct splash when Jimmy Staton's feet went back into the bottom of the boat. Tubby felt downwards.

A moment later he made the air tingle with as sulphurous an assortment of oaths as any Billingsgate fishmonger had ever used.

"What's up?" Stan had his back to Tubby, and did not know the Geordie had stopped rowing.

"Up!" Tubby roared, bending to lift Staton to a sitting position. "Nothing's up, man—nothing at all. Only we've a couple of inches of water over the boards, and it's rising fast.

CHAPTER THIRTEEN

DISASTER!

THORSON's devilish scheme was working perfectly. As Stan and Tubby tried to locate the "leak," more wads of paper were washed out of the holes and the flow of water increased.

"I've found one hole," Tubby snorted.

"I've found two," Stan told him. "And . . . yes, there's another one, Tubby . . ."

"Don't tell me," Tubby growled, grabbing his oar, "pull like blazes."

Within half a minute they bumped against an ice-pan, and Stan scrambled on to it, while Tubby straddled his legs to keep the boat from rocking.

Staton was dragged on to the ice, then the two boxes of stores were salvaged.

"Can we save the boat?" Stan asked. "We might be able to plug the holes."

The ice-pan rocked crazily as the two Britishers struggled to get the water-logged boat out of the water, and by the time they had accomplished the rescue work they were both perspiring.

Stan untied Jimmy Staton's gag, then loosened the knots on his wrist bonds.

"I tried to stop you taking this boat," Jimmy said, rubbing his sore jaws. "I didn't know what Thorson had done to it, but I knew—he didn't mean—to let you get away alive."

"You rat!" Tubby Fenner grabbed Staton by the throat, but Stan separated them.

"There's enough damage been done for one night, Tubby. Lay off."

"I said he'd double-cross us," Tubby roared. "Him and his offer of help."

"Well, look in the boxes," Staton gulped, rubbing his throat. "If I'd meant you to die, I needn't have packed any stores. You are to blame, Fenner. I wanted you to have the port boat."

From the box containing spare clothing they got a change for Staton, and dry sea-boot stockings for themselves. Then they inspected the boat by the light of a candle. This was no easy task, for the wind was now blowing gustily, bringing occasional flurries of snow.

With the boat turned over, they could see how thorough Thorson had been. Twenty inch-diameter holes had been bored in the planking and the paper plugs had washed out of eight.

"If I lay hands on that swine——" Tubby began bitterly, but stopped when Stan said sharply:

"Stow that, Tubby, let's think now; the wind's blowing up for a storm."

"There was a gale warning on the weather report," Jimmy Staton confirmed Stan's prediction, then added: "You know what that means."

After a short silence Stan asked:

"Could we get back to the *Bear*?" and he looked anxiously for some sign of the ship they had left.

"There's a light over there," Staton had stood up and was now pointing into the inky darkness. "I thought I saw a green spot a moment ago."

They stared in the direction indicated, but snow and sleet, driving down, limited visibility to a score of yards. Before they could see anything they had to sit down hurriedly for a sudden screaming gust made the ice-pan rock uneasily.

Staton, however, was on his feet a minute later, peering anxiously into the darkness, and once again he insisted he had seen a light.

For the second time the two friends got up to look, and for the second time, saw nothing.

"I did see it," Jimmy Staton insisted, "I'll go across. I've got a torch in my pocket, and if I reach her——"

Tubby Fenner laughed scornfully, and jerked Staton down to the ice.

"If you've got a torch my lad, you're not taking it with you. I trust you no farther than I could throw a rhinoceros."

"I could make that ship in half an hour," Staton argued. "If you lit a fire at the end of an hour, to guide me, I'd bring a rescue party."

"And everybody would live happy ever after," Tubby jeered. "Listen, matey, when we move, we move together. Is there any reason why we shouldn't?"

"Only that I have spent two seasons working on the ice," was the cool retort. "I know something about it—you don't. In this storm you'd be in the water in five minutes."

"We'll stick together, just the same," Tubby insisted. "I'd never forgive myself, Mr. Staton, if you went off alone, and had an accident. You might even wander back to the *Bear*, by mistake. That'd be terrible for you."

He had to shout, for the wind was gusting furiously, then dropping, only to rise again in a threatening scream.

Staton rose to his feet.

"All right," he shouted. "We'll go together, but if anybody falls into the water, I hope it's you."

"Another crack like that, mister, and I'll belt that sarcasm out of you," Tubby bawled.

"Lead the way, Jimmy," Stan suggested, picking up one of the boxes, "the longer we stay here, the less hope there is."

Tubby bent to pick up the other box. Jimmy Staton produced his torch, switched it on, and flashed the light full into the eyes of his two companions. The brilliance dazzled them and Tubby lifted a hand to shield himself.

Then Jimmy Stanton turned and ran.

Tubby dropped his box just as Stan began to run and the two friends collided. Stan slipped and

Tubby fell with him. By the time they had sorted themselves out, Staton had vanished. He had gone nimbly from one ice-pan to the next, and the night had swallowed him completely.

"Well, that's the fellow you wanted to save from a life of crime," Tubby roared. "Tchah! If ever you've been a sucker, Stan, it's now. I told you he'd double-cross us."

In his heart of hearts, Stan agreed, but he tried to defend his own judgment.

"Give him time," he pleaded. "One man has a better chance of getting to the ship than three. We'll make ourselves comfortable in the boat, and I'll light a fire in about an hour."

"You make me weep," Tubby ranted, crawling under the upturned boat. "You'll stop trusting that crook when he's put a bullet through your head. You haven't got the sense you were born with. If he saw a light it was from the *Bear*. While we're keeping nice and cosy here, he'll be having a glass of whisky with Thorson, celebrating our departure to hell—or wherever people go who freeze to death."

Miserably silent, Stan followed his friend under the boat. They propped one gunwale up with the two boxes, and crouched there while the storm grew in fury, forcing them to brace their backs against the boat to prevent the wind flinging it over them.

Their ice-floe rocked uneasily. The whole ice-field was bobbing and heaving. The wind was intermittent, whistling with all the fury of a tornado, then dying to a zephyr, only to spring up again with renewed violence.

In the midst of it all, Tubby apologised to Stan.

"Sorry about losing my wool!" he shouted. "I'm not really blaming you. It just makes me mad to think of Staton getting away. The crooks always seem to kick off with an advantage. Folks try to help 'em, and they take advantage of it."

Stan merely nodded, though no man could have seen his nod. The night was like pitch, and blacker still under the boat.

They sat and shivered, trying not to think of what lay ahead. An Arctic storm often lasted for days. If this one lasted a day they were doomed.

How long they were there, slowly growing colder, more stiff, more mentally numbed by the shrieking wind, neither knew; then Stan suddenly saw a thin pink line on the ice at his feet. A light! The ruddy light from a torch!

Stan shouted, and dug Tubby in the ribs, but the "Geordie" muttered sleepily. He was in that state of freezing when pain and cold are replaced by comfortable lassitude.

Stan's brain was muddled but he realised a light meant human beings, and somehow he got from beneath the boat.

Snow was falling. The wind had died completely during the past five minutes, and there was a thick covering of white over everything. The upturned boat looked like any other small ice-hummock. If Stan had not gone out when he did, the search party would have passed on, without realising they had overlooked their objective.

Someone shouted. A rifle was fired into the air to warn the rest of the party that the search was ended. Staton had kept his promise.

Stan and Tubby were dosed with rum, and half-carried, half-dragged across the gently heaving field of ice-pans, reaching a small Norwegian sealing ship about a mile away.

Tubby Fenner had just one moment of lucidity. Along with Stan he had been taken into the captain's cabin and there they had been rubbed and pummelled with hot towels. They had been smacked and punched until the blood was circulating again.

Tubby opened his eyes when hot coffee was put to his lips. He looked about for a moment in utter bewilderment, then his eyes focused on Jimmy Staton. An expression of blank amazement showed on his face. He blinked, looked about, then whispered:

"You—came back!"

Staton grinned.

"Yes—I came back," he admitted.

"Hm! I—was wrong," Tubby whispered, his eyes beginning to close again, and in a voice which was little more than a sigh, he finished: "Sorry—Staton—misjudged you."

"What does he say?" the Norwegian skipper asked.

"He's thanking you," Jimmy lied.

"They have both been near to death," the Norwegian said, "I think they will thank you very much when they recover."

Staton smiled a peculiar smile and helped Tubby and Stan into bunks.

The storm lasted for thirty-six hours. It put a two-foot blanket of snow over everything, then laid siege to men and ships with a fall in temperature which locked the ice-floes into one solid field.

Stan Farrager was up and about at the end of twenty-four hours. Tubby lay in his bunk, pale and shaken. He had just missed an attack of pneumonia. Whisky and seal fat in liberal quantities had prevented congestion of the lungs, but the Geordie had to keep to his bunk.

About noon on the second day, a pale sun gave promise of at least a few hours of fine weather.

The captain of the sealer, a bearded Norwegian of the old school, climbed to his crow's nest to see if there were other sealers in the vicinity. He and Stan had had a long talk about the *Bear*, and the mission she was on.

Had he possessed a radio, the Norwegian would have broadcast the news of Thorson, but his ship was forty years old. There was no electricity aboard and he carried only a small receiving set, worked from batteries, just capable of getting weather reports. There was no way of getting a message outside.

The moment he could get under way, the Norwegian intended to contact one of the more modern sealers, and get her to wireless the Norwegian authorities, asking for help.

Until a gunboat arrived he hoped to get the sealers to work close together. This would prevent Thorson picking off ship after ship, safe from intervention.

"We are all well armed—as far as rifles go," the Norwegian had insisted, "and together we could withstand the attack of a dozen ships like the *Bear*."

On deck, Stan watched the Norwegian climb nimbly to the crow's nest. He saw him lift a pair of glasses and scan the horizon. It was when he looked to the west he paused, and stared for a long time. Then he called down to Stan.

"What kind of vessel was this Russian ship? The real one, I mean? There is a vessel coming through the ice towards us—and she is flying the Russian flag. She has one gun on her foredeck, and it looks as if she has others aft. Come up and look. You will know her, I'm sure. I haven't seen either the real Russian, nor yet this *Bear* you told me of."

Stan went up the ratlines, and Sigurd Gundorf, the skipper of the sealer, handed him the glasses; but by the time he had focused them, a third

man had climbed up to the crow's nest—Jimmy
Staton.

Stan looked long and earnestly at the approaching vessel. She was punching her way through
the ice, her bows sending a spray of ice chips
flying on either side, and it struck him then that
he had never seen the *Bear* from a distance. When
he had gone aboard her in Tromso he had been
unconscious. When he had left her, it had been
night-time.

"It's the *Bear* all right," Jimmy Staton supplied
the information. "I could tell the cut of her jib
anywhere."

"So!" Sigurd Gundorf looked at his two guests,
and shrugged. "What now? I am a prisoner until
the warmer weather loosens the ice. My ship is
old, and not powerful enough to break out of the
ice just yet."

Stan said nothing, and Jimmy Staton merely
shrugged. There was nothing they could say.
It was the Norwegian who put their fears into
words.

"If this Captain Thorson boards me, what will
happen? Me he will rob, of course; but what
will he do to you? He is a desperate man, eh?
Not anxious to leave any one behind who could
give evidence against him. It is bad, eh?"

"You're dead right," Staton agreed, then volunteered a suggestion: "I suggest we all go out for
seals. Farrager and I can stay away from the
ship until the *Bear* moves off."

Just then there was a yell from the deck. The mate of the sealer announced that the approaching ship was signalling them. Stan focused the glasses again. A string of flags had been run up. They were international code flags, and meant nothing to Stan, who was an engineer.

They scrambled to the deck where the mate was already consulting the "book of words." Laboriously he spelled out the message:

"Stand by for inspection of ship and crew. I am boarding you."

Jimmy Staton raised his eyebrows.

"That washes out my idea of getting away," he said slowly. "It looks as if you'll meet Thorson again."

"Yes," Stan agreed.

"Too bad!" Staton turned away and felt for a cigarette. Silently the crew of the sealer watched the *Bear* come closer. She made a splendid picture. Her bows crunched the ice as if it had been no more than icing sugar. A dozen men in smart naval uniform lined her starboard rail, while a man in immaculate blue, with gold facings on cap and cuffs, stood on the starboard wing of the bridge. She was the pirate *par excellence* and could pass as a bona fide gunboat-patrol ship almost anywhere.

Stan watched her, fascinated. There was no hope of evading Thorson. For one thing, Tubby Fenner was below in a bunk. He could not hide.

There was a sudden great threshing of water

at the stern of the *Bear* as her phosphor bronze screws went into reverse. The ice at her bows ceased to spray, and finally the boil of water stopped flooding along her lean flanks as the screws ceased churning.

The *Bear* was hove-to.

CHAPTER FOURTEEN

PRISON SHIP

THE boarding operations were carried out with the slickness one might have expected from a well-drilled man o' war crew. A rope ladder was swung over the rail, and a party of armed seamen scrambled down to the ice. Falling into line smartly, they marched through the deep snow to the sealer, and climbed aboard.

Sigurd Gundorf moved along the deck to meet them, and began to protest, insisting that his ship was in international waters and therefore not subject to inspection by a Russian warship.

Thorson's mate, Igorsky, thrust his face within inches of Sigurd and sneered:

"All these waters are Russian. When you get back to Norway you can make as many complaints as you like. While we are aboard, Captain, it will pay you to be polite. Resistance will be met with more than impoliteness." He grinned as he mouthed that last word.

In silence the sealers and bogus Russians waited for Thorson. When he came he was resplendent in immaculate uniform, a sword trailing at his side, and he carried himself with all the aplomb one would have expected of a high-ranking naval officer.

He climbed aboard, assisted by two Finns; then Sigurd Gundorf was brought along to him, and Thorson's first question made Stan realise the game was up.

"I am looking for three men, Captain. Three Britishers. They are wanted by my Government. Have you seen them? They have no papers to prove their identity, and are from a British ship."

Sigurd Gundorf made a noise in his throat which suggested anger and impatience, but with a great effort he kept his temper, and said:

"Since you have violated International Law, sir, I refuse to give you any help at all, and I assure you that——"

"All right, cut the rest," Thorson snapped, and turned to look at the assembled sealers.

Gundorf's crew were lined against the rail, and Thorson and his mate began their inspection immediately. It was cursory enough, for every man of Sigurd Gundorf's crew was bearded. Stan and Tubby, if not exactly clean shaven, would only have a couple of days' growth on their cheeks.

While Stan waited, he felt a hand close over the fingers of his right hand.

"So long, Stan." It was Jimmy Staton, and a moment later he stepped out of line, and walked towards Thorson.

Thorson looked up and Staton nodded.

"I wondered how long it would be before I was rescued," he began. "We got here the same night —and darned lucky to do it, too."

Thorson turned without a word and walked to the stern. Staton followed him, watched by every one on deck. They talked for about ten minutes and when the conversation came to an end both men were smiling. They walked along the deck until they reached Stan Farrager. Then Thorson frowned, and turned to Staton. He was in high spirits.

"I seem to have seen this young man before, Jimmee. I turn this way—and I bump into him. I turn that way—and he pops around a corner." He was thoroughly enjoying the situation. Then, in a sharper tone, "Where is your fat friend?"

"He's in a cabin, a sick man," Stan replied. "You almost succeeded, Mr. Thorson, and I shan't forget that boat when I give evidence in court."

"Tut-tut," Thorson mocked, "you shouldn't harbour ill-feelings. Life is a game . . . sometimes we win, sometimes we lose."

"You are going to lose," Stan was stung to retort. "You've just about had your time, y'know."

"Ah-ha. Been talking, eh? What've you told this old fool . . . Gundorf?"

Thorson did not know that Sigurd Gundorf was just behind him, and the sealer captain was stung to instant reply: the contempt in Thorson's voice making him flush with anger.

"The old fool, Gundorf, knows everything, Mr. Thorson," Sigurd snarled, "so you can forget your pose as a Russian naval officer. You thief!"

"Please . . . please," Thorson turned and held up his hands in mock horror. "Thief! No, no. I shall not touch one of your skins, Captain. I promise you that."

"You won't?" There was relief and disbelief in Sigurd Gundorf's voice. Then the old man's eyes flashed with anger as Thorson threw back his head and laughed uproariously.

"No, Captain. *I* do not touch sealskins, but I am afraid *you* will. You and your crew are to load all your catch into my holds."

"I refuse," Gundorf snapped, "and my men will refuse. I'll see you roasting in hell before I——" He stopped, for Thorson's mate had jabbed him smartly in the back with the muzzle of an automatic.

"Don't be too stupid," Thorson mocked. "My mate has an itchy trigger finger. I'll save you the indignity of handling the skins. You can superintend the work."

Gundorf's face was white with anger as he turned away. Then Thorson recalled him.

"By the way, Captain, when you have emptied the hold of skins you can tranship your stores: food, cartridges, etc. I shall need them all."

"My stores!" Gundorf blanched. "My stores? How am I to feed my men?"

"Don't worry about that," Thorson jibed, "I

shall feed them. As you know so much about
me . . . I must take you with me. I should hate
you to spread the news that the *Bear* is not really
a Russian ship. It would make all the other
sealing skippers most angry."

"But what is to happen to me and my ship?"
Gundorf asked. In the past minute he seemed to
have aged twenty years, as if he knew what the
answer would be, although hoping against hope
he was wrong.

"You will come aboard the *Bear* as my guest,"
Thorson replied, and laughed cynically as he
added: "As for your ship—she is very old, and
I think she would like to rest on the sea bed with
Davy Jones."

Gundorf almost got his hands on Thorson's
throat, but the mate's pistol stretched him out on
the icy deck, a trickle of blood on his temple.

For one moment it looked as if the sealers might
defy Thorson's pirates, but a shot over their heads
calmed them. Threatened by a dozen guns they
had no option but obey orders, and the tranship-
ment of the cargo of sealskins began at once.

For the next four hours the two ships were a-
bustle with activity. The frozen sculps were
brought up on deck in bales of a dozen, carted
across the snow, and stowed in the capacious holds
of the *Bear*.

Stan had to help with the work, and he ached
from head to foot by the time everything, including food and stores, had been transferred. Then

Thorson allowed his crew to pillage whatever they fancied from the ship.

When they finally returned to the *Bear* night had fallen, though it was not as dark as other nights. A sickle moon had risen, and her pale rays reflecting from the snow and ice threw a ghastly pallor over the scene.

Stan, who had been put in a small hold with the crew of the sealer, was called on deck. Escorted by two armed men he was led to the rail where Thorson was smoking a cheroot.

"I thought I would let you see something which few living men have seen," Thorson said, pointing to Gundorf's vessel. "Doubtless you read stories of pirates when you were a boy. I did, and loved them." Stan remained silent, wondering what was coming.

Thorson turned and blew a wisp of smoke into Stan's face.

"Come, Mr. Farrager," he prompted, "why so despondent? You are going to see something which would make headlines throughout the world. You are going to see the scuttling of a ship."

"Have you no pity?" Stan asked. "That ship is Gundorf's life. He's been telling me how he worked his way up from an ordinary sealing hand to this—master of his own vessel."

"Whatever happens to Gundorf is your fault, Mr. Farrager," Thorson said coldly, "I asked you to join me—and you laughed at me. Through you—I have had to take Gundorf and his crew prisoner. I can't set you free. Or, at least, I am going to set you all free, which may sound like a riddle."

"I'd like the answer," Stan suggested.

"You shall have it," Thorson threw his half-smoked cheroot on to the ice. "From here I am sailing north. The spring is coming. Maybe I shall meet just one or two sealing ships. I need about four thousand skins more. When I have got them, I am going as far north as the ice will let me. Then I shall put you all out to fend for yourselves. If you get back—good luck to you!"

Before Stan could find an answer there was a sudden, rumbling explosion somewhere in Gundorf's vessel. The deck amidships split wide open. A great tongue of flame licked upwards, throwing into vivid relief the crow's nest, the long thin funnel, already beginning to fall over the side, and revealing pieces of debris shooting upwards. The ship was broken in half by the explosion.

The bows and stern lifted skywards, then, even while their eyes were still dazzled by the glare of the explosion, Sigurd Gundorf's little sealer vanished beneath the tossing, ice-covered water.

The darkness which followed was like a black curtain. A minute earlier there had been a ship, bathed in pale moonlight; now there was nothing.

"You can go below," Thorson said, and for a

moment Stan fancied that even he, murderer of a ship, was slightly subdued.

"Listen, Thorson," Stan said, resisting the effort of the nearest guard to move him, "you've got forty men below—men who have done nothing against you. Men with wives and families——"

"Go below," Thorson ordered, but Stan still clung to the rail.

"Put me and Tubby on the ice, if you must," he went on, "but don't murder Gundorf's crew. If you——"

Thorson said something to the men who were holding on to Stan, and they jerked the Britisher away from the rail. As they were dragging him away Stan heard Thorson give his last word on the subject.

"It's all or none, Farrager. It's got to be all."

CHAPTER FIFTEEN

NO MERCY

For six days Stan Farrager, Tubby Fenner, and the crew of the scuttled sealer, were kept prisoner in one of the smaller holds of the *Bear*. Tubby Fenner had a mattress, because he had been ill, but no one else had a bed. Fortunately the *Bear* was steam heated, and no great hardship was suffered.

Seven times in those six days the *Bear* intercepted sealers, and confiscated the catches of skins.

Twice, Thorson was lucky not to be intercepted by the Russian patrol ship which was still prowling about, checking every sealer in the hope of tracing the vessel which had fired on her in the White Sea and then escaped.

Each evening the prisoners were allowed on deck for an hour's exercise, going up in batches of seven. Tubby Fenner never went up, for though he was quite fit again, he had decided it might pay him to pretend to be still an invalid.

When every available inch of space in the *Bear's* holds was crammed with stolen sealskins, Thorson headed for the ice-pack into which sealers did not normally venture.

The days were growing perceptibly longer, the sun rising earlier and setting later. Flocks of migrant birds, the hardiest of them all, were already beginning to pass over on their way to the summer mating grounds on Bear Island. Spring was in the air: Spring which would bring a quick break-up of the outer rim of the ice-pack. There would be a period of violent storms, then calm and sunshine, followed by more storms, and the hitherto solid pack-ice would become broken floes, swiftly melting.

Towards this ice rim Thorson headed the *Bear*.

On the evening of that first day of northward steaming, the usual armed guard appeared at supper time, escorting Ben and three others, carrying dishes of food.

The dishes were set down and the guards withdrew. Then one of the Norwegians dipped a ladle into the great mound of mashed potatoes. He put potatoes on three plates, but his fourth ladleful contained something solid . . . something which toppled back into the big pan.

Grunts of disgust turned to cries of amazement as the man with the ladle, gingerly picking up the strangely solid ' potato,' dropped it on to the floor. It was something wrapped in greaseproof paper. When the paper was taken off, it revealed an automatic pistol.

The gun was handed to Sigurd Gundorf while a dozen voices drew his attention to something stuffed into the muzzle.

"Stand back!" Gundorf ordered. "It's maybe another of Thorson's devilish tricks."

The circle about Gundorf widened at that, and in a solemn silence the bearded Norwegian drew from the barrel a slim roll of paper. In the same breathless silence the men watched their captain unroll the paper, and read what was written; Gundorf held out the paper to Stan.

"It is for you. From Mr. Staton."

"From Staton!" Stan shot a quick glance at Tubby.

"Probably a trick," Tubby grunted.

Stan read the note, while Gundorf translated to his men.

"Stan Farrager," he read. "The cook will let you have this gun. It is fully loaded. What you can do, I don't know. Thorson intends to maroon you—a few at a time, at different points. He has no intention of any of you getting back alive. If I can do anything to help I will; but don't depend on me. Thorson doesn't trust me. Keep your eyes skinned."

The silence which followed lasted about half a minute, then there was a babel of voices, silenced quickly by Gundorf.

"Do you want Thorson to know something has happened?" he demanded sternly, "there may be a guard on the other side of the door. Be silent, every one!"

They obeyed, and waited. They knew the North

well enough, and they knew that if Thorson did maroon them on the fringe of the ice-pack, it meant death. There would be no walking to safety. Once on that desolate wilderness of ice, they were as remote from help as if they had been at the North Pole itself.

"Better to die fighting in this hold, than be put out on ice," one bearded veteran snarled. "Who'll fight by my side?"

"We have *one* gun," Stan said pointedly, "let's not do anything rash. Something might turn up."

No one believed him. They had discussed Thorson and his mad venture from every possible angle. His success depended on two things . . . disposing of his stolen catch and preventing any description of himself and the *Bear* from leaking out. Up to now the sealers he had robbed believed him to be a Russian gunboat. Thorson could not, therefore, let his prisoners get back alive.

The non-appearance of any war vessels suggested that the message sent out by Stan from the *Bear* had not reached any vital ship. Possibly it had been picked up, but as it was not repeated, might have been taken for a hoax.

The prisoners discussed the situation over their meal and long into the night. Yet no man could think of any plan which offered the slightest hope of success. One automatic pistol was little better than useless against Thorson's well-armed crew.

Thorson kept the *Bear* punching her way

through the ice all night. When morning came they were grinding into real ice-fields. They could hear the cracking screech every few minutes as the ship's bows forced open a lane. Later there were increasing occasions when the ship was stopped, reversed, then put forward again . . . to charge some particularly tough stretch of ice.

After breakfast the mate came down and ordered six men out on deck. One of the ways suggested of defeating Thorson had been a mass refusal to do anything. This was now tried. No man moved.

The mate slipped back the safety catch on his big automatic.

"I am going to count three," he said, speaking in Norwegian, "if you are not moving then, I shall shoot you through the knee. It ought to be painful there. One . . . two . . ."

There was no disobeying a threat like that. Nor did any one blame the man concerned for getting up and walking slowly out and up on deck. Five others obeyed, after being threatened in like manner.

"You needn't worry," the mate said, grinning. "We're putting you off with plenty of food. You'll soon be picked up."

"The ice-pack is already beginning to break up," Gundorf protested. "Each day will mean marching farther north as the ice melts; each day we have less chance of getting out alive."

The mate laughed and slammed the door.

At the end of about five minutes the *Bear* backed out of the lane she had made, and steamed for another hour. A further six men were then put out on the ice. Thorson was putting the prisoners out at distances of seven or eight miles apart—hoping thus to keep them separated.

At length there were only five men left: Tubby, still lying on his mattress, and pretending to be too sick to move; Stan Farrager, Sigurd Gundorf, and two of his crew.

Then once more the door of the hold opened and the mate stood there, grinning.

"Come on!" he ordered, "we always keep the best to the last."

Very slowly four of the five rose to their feet. Tubby Fenner remained where he was. When the mate bellowed to him to get up, the burly Geordie shook his head.

"Sorry," he whispered, "you'll have to count me out. I can't move, and that's that."

Gundorf and Stan were ordered to help Tubby up on deck and they made their way slowly up the narrow companionway. As they went up, a step at a time, Stan whispered:

"I'm not going over the side without a fight, Tubby. When I ease you to the deck, lie flat and keep your fingers crossed. I've never shot a man before, but it's them or us——" He did not finish his sentence. He knew if they got out alive, it would be by some unexpected miracle. One gun would not save them.

Watched as if they had been desperate criminals, the five prisoners were ushered on deck. They had not seen daylight for a week, and the ice glare was almost blinding in its intensity. For a few moments they huddled together, blinking like owls.

Thorson was standing amidships, and just behind him, Jimmy Staton. When the five men had been ushered closer Thorson broke the silence.

"This, gentlemen, is where we part company. I don't like to do it—but you must admit, your presence would be an embarrassment once we got back to friendlier waters. If you would like to go first, Mr. Farrager, I'll see that your fat friend is helped over with all the care at our command. I don't like losing you—you have the makings of a good diesel engineer."

"Have you no conscience?" Stan asked, starting to lower Tubby to the deck, and doing it in such a way that Tubby acted as a shield for his right hand, which was groping for the automatic.

"Conscience!" Thorson laughed at the idea, "I cannot afford such a luxury. When you—drop that!"

Stan was upright, the automatic free and ready for action.

Crack!

The shot was unexpected, for Stan was only lifting his gun, when it was shot out of his hand. With his usual thoroughness, Thorson had posted a gunman on top of the deckhousing, and it was that man, half hidden behind a ventilator, who had fired.

The bullet scored Stan Farrager's knuckles, and for a moment he stood staring dazedly at the ugly weal on the back of his hand. It was a 'picture' shot, disarming him without really damaging him.

Then Jimmy Staton acted. He rammed a gun into Thorson's back, and shouted:

"Stand still, everybody. If there's a move Thorson gets it. Drop your guns! Come on, Thorson . . . tell 'em. You get one through the spine if you don't."

For ten long seconds which seemed to stretch into minutes, no one moved and no one spoke. Staton jabbed Thorson again, and he winced.

"Tell them, Thorson! I'm in charge . . . it's you or me, now—and I've got the gun."

Thorson's mouth opened spasmodically, but no sound came. The tables had been turned so swiftly he was unable to think.

"You on the deckhousing," Jimmy Staton ordered, "drop your gun and come down."

The man dropped the gun, then turned and dropped to the deck. He rolled over and was on his knees with a gun in his hand before Jimmy Staton realised it.

Crack . . . crack!

If Staton had been standing directly behind Thorson he would have been completely protected; but he had moved slightly to one side. It was enough. Thorson had chosen the gunman for his accurate marksmanship.

Jimmy Staton sagged, the gun dropped from his hand, and he went down, almost pushing Thorson off balance in doing so.

At once Stan Farrager and Tubby Fenner moved, leaping for the door leading to the engine-room. It was a now-or-never effort, while Thorson and his men were still too stupefied to do anything.

CHAPTER SIXTEEN

A SEA-COOK LEAVES HIS DUFF

THE sudden disappearance of Stan Farrager and Tubby Fenner through the door which led to the engine-room, shook Thorson's men to life.

A perfect fusillade of bullets splintered the woodwork, banging the door shut. It gave the two Britishers those few extra moments which saved them. When the first of the Finns jerked open the door, there was no sign of either Stan or Tubby.

Stan went down the almost vertical steel ladders like a circus clown, and the bump as his feet hit the engine-room plates shook him to the crown of his head.

Tubby took his feet off the rungs and kept his hands on the rails. The Geordie had gone into so many engine-rooms at speed, it came second nature to slide down that way.

"Out o' the way, man," Tubby gasped, grabbing Stan and whipping him towards the stern. "Did you bring the gun with you?"

Stan managed to grunt he was not a superman and the automatic was still on deck.

"Can't be helped," Tubby growled. "Get

through to the propeller shaft tunnel. I want
some iron between me and those idiots."

Bang . . . clank!

Someone had got through the top door and
fired. The bullet went wide, but the metallic
clang as it struck a bulkhead plate was warning
that there would be no kid-glove methods from
now on.

Once in the propeller shaft tunnel, they both
stopped, gasping. Tubby felt for the light switch
and a moment later the dusty light bulb was
throwing a yellow glimmer over them and the
shimmering steel propeller shaft at their feet.

"Now, what?" Tubby panted, wiping his brow,
and leaving a smear of cobweb dirt across his eyebrows. "We're safe for the moment—about as
safe as the fellow who grabbed the lion's tail. If
we'd a gun we'd be all right. We've only this door
and the trapdoor to watch."

Stan looked up instinctively. A narrow iron
ladder ran up the bulkhead wall which divided
the port propeller shaft from the starboard shaft.
In the roof was a small trapdoor, giving access to
a storeroom up above. Beyond that was another
storeroom, and then the deck.

Instead of answering, Stan cupped his hands
about his mouth, and shouted:

"Yes, come on—there's a bullet for the first
man!"

"Where are they?" Tubby whispered.

"I could feel the vibration on this plate," Stan whispered. The plate on which he stood went through to the engine-room, and he had felt it quiver a little as a man on the other side of the door put his weight on it.

"I hope he understood you," Tubby said, then chuckled. "Man, you've got a powerful imagination. What'll you shoot him with?"

Stan pulled a wry face. There were times when he wished Tubby would not try to be funny.

In the silence which followed they waited. They could hear someone shouting angrily. The words came faintly but there was no mistaking the speaker. It was Thorson, an angry Thorson.

"We're trapped in here, y'know," Stan said quietly, "they could lock us in and starve us to death." He looked up at the trapdoor in the ceiling.

"Try it," Tubby suggested, "I'll keep 'em talking. If the way's clear—we'll make a bolt for it."

Stan climbed the steel ladder as quietly as he could, while Tubby began to shout threats through the crack where the door met its iron supports.

The trapdoor lifted easily enough, and the room smelled strongly of sealskins. Stan squeezed through, found the door and opened it. Next moment he slammed it shut. The passage into which he had peeped had changed from blackness to glaring light. A man with an automatic had come into the passage and switched on the light.

The door could be locked, but not bolted, and as Stan had no key, it was retreat or be caught. For a moment he toyed with the idea of trying the ladder which led to the storeroom above, but decided it was too risky. If he succeeded, it meant he and Tubby would be separated.

Back he went through the trapdoor, and down the ladder.

"No go?" Tubby asked, and Stan shook his head, then told him what had happened.

"Well, I've just about one pipe of baccy," Tubby said, feeling for his flat pouch, "I'll have a last smoke—and then—we'll see."

"I wish I knew what we would see," Stan growled, pacing back and forward like a caged lion. "We made a real box-up of the whole business. If only I'd spotted that chap on the cabin top——"

"Stop worrying," Tubby advised, looking regretfully at the meagre collection of tobacco dust he had poured into his pipe. "It's a forlorn hope, anyway. Though I'll never forget Thorson's face when Jimmy Staton stuck that gun into his back."

"Yes, you owe him an apology—if we ever get the chance of offering it to him."

Tubby struck a match, and puffed with obvious enjoyment. He carefully tamped down the pathetic pipeful, then nodded.

"Yeah, Stan, when I'm wrong, I'll admit it. He tried —and you can't do more than that."

There was silence for a few minutes, then came the sound of voices from the storeroom above.

"Thorson," Stan whispered, and went quietly up the ladder. He heard Thorson's plug-ugly mate say something about the Britishers being armed. Thorson grunted disdainfully:

"All right, keep watch. I'll soon have them out."

Footsteps, then silence.

Stan went down the ladder, and repeated what he had heard. Tubby raised his eyebrows, and said:

"Well, if Thorson says he'll soon have us out, Stan—we'll soon be out. I've got a healthy respect for that man. When he says he'll do something—it takes something big to stop him."

"If only we were armed," Stan whispered.

"Yeah. 'If wishes were horses, beggars would ride,'" Tubby chuckled, then more soberly, "I don't know how Thorson will get us out—but I've got a feeling we've had it."

The minutes dragged. Both Britishers were listening anxiously. If there was a devilish way of getting them out of this impregnable rat-hole, Thorson would think of it.

Thorson did not disappoint them.

There was a faint squeak from above. They looked up, but could see nothing. Then, visible as little silver streaks in the light, something began to drip down on them.

Plop . . . plop . . . plop . . . plop.

The drops were steady, persistent, but for a few moments there was nothing to indicate what this meant.

"Upset his cup of tea," Tubby said facetiously, "I hope he isn't trying to drown us out. He'll have a——" Tubby sniffed suspiciously, then bent over the little wet spots on the floor. He got a drop of whatever was falling on the back of his neck, and wiped it off swiftly as he straightened up.

There was no necessity to explain. Stan had already got the first nose-tingling whiff: *ammonia!*

A moment later the trapdoor was lifted, and down came a bottle. It crashed like a bomb, splashing ammonia about, and at once Tubby and Stan were coughing and gasping as the fumes caught their throats.

Part of the equipment of the *Bear* was a refrigerating plant, for the ship had been used in the Middle East in pre-war days, and it was from the refrigerating machinery Thorson had got his ammonia.

In less than two minutes the unequal battle was over. Choking, half-strangled by the fumes,

Tubby and Stan pushed their way out into the engine-room. Four men were waiting, and they rushed forward, only to retreat even more quickly as clouds of ammonia fumes met them, striking at friend and foe alike.

Had the two Britishers been in better shape they might have benefited from this temporary set-back, but they were past taking advantage of anything. They wanted fresh air—air for the eyes, air for their lungs and throats. They reeled drunkenly across the engine-room, and crawled weakly up on to the deck.

Thorson and his mate were waiting, and they roared with laughter. Stan and Tubby were a pitiable spectacle. Their eyes were red and streaming, and they were gasping for air.

Jimmy Staton was propped against the ship's rail, his face was deathly white. He stared at Stan and Tubby but no smile crossed his countenance.

"Now will you believe me when I say that I plan thoroughly," Thorson gloated. "You can't beat me."

Neither Stan nor Tubby answered. They sat on the ice-covered deck, mopping their eyes, breathing deep of the cold, clean air, and feeling too shaken to care what Thorson said or did.

While they were recovering, Sigurd Gundorf and his two men were marched out of a cabin by the cook. Ben looked rather ridiculous. He held a heavy automatic in his right hand, a cleaning cloth in the other, and his shabby chef's cap was still perched awkwardly on his mop of grey hair.

The Norwegains looked downcast at sight of Stan and Tubby. They had hoped the two Britishers might have averted the threat of marooning.

"Now, Messrs. Farrager and Fenner," Thorson jeered, "we'll get on with the business. Perhaps you would condescend to climb over the rail."

As Stan got to his feet, Jimmy Staton called weakly across.

"I'd . . . like to . . . speak to you . . . for a moment, Stan," and turning to Thorson he asked humbly: "May I "

There was hate in Thorson's eyes as he looked at his one-time partner.

"Yes, you rat. Say what you like, but be quick."

Stan walked across to Staton, and kneeling, asked gently:

"Are you badly hurt, Jimmy?"

"Never mind that," Staton croaked, "Stan, I've made a mess of things. I did try to help you."

"'Course you did," Stan soothed. "Everything will work out right in the end."

"Oh, I know," Staton managed a crooked little smile. "It always does—in the story books. Stan —will you believe me when I say—I'm sorry."

"Of course I believe you!" There was something about Staton's eyes which told Stan that his one-time pal was dying.

"Yes . . . you do," Jimmy Staton said. "Will you . . . do something for me, Stan? Tell them back home how I died. Will you?"

Stan nodded. No use trying to persuade Jimmy Staton he was not dying. It was written on his face.

"Thanks." Jimmy Staton lifted his left hand, and now that crooked little smile was there again: "I'd like to have the left handshake, Stan. Just for old times' sake."

They shook hands.

Then Thorston shouted angrily:

"Come on, Mr. Farrager—we're wasting time."

Stan moved, and as he did so Jimmy Staton's right hand came up, and there was a gun in it. Thorson died instantaneously. The broken-nosed mate fired twice before he fell, dropping across Thorson.

One of the Finn guards fired at Staton. Then Ben, the cook, dropped to one knee and began to pump bullets into the little knot of Finns and Lapps. Four men went down with leg wounds before the rest scattered.

"There's a time for cookin', and a time for shootin'," Ben said grimly. "I reckons it's shootin' time now. You stay here."

"Where are you going, you fool?" Tubby roared, stooping to collect a gun, "you'll . . ."

"You stay under cover, Mister," Ben ordered, "I've some scores to settle, if them scum feels like shootin'."

Stan went across to Jimmy, but Staton had crossed the final border, and in his last few moments had atoned for some of his sins. In dying he had taken Thorson and the mate with him.

The Finns, Lapps and Poles who made up the crew of the *Bear* were completely demoralised by Thorson's death. Ben disarmed them, confined them to the fo'castle, and locked them there.

Captain Gundorf took command, and three days were spent combing the fringe of the ice-pack for the remainder of his crew. Not one man was lost. Then they set course for North Cape, and Tromso.

Two hours before they dropped anchor Ben sought out Stan Farrager.

"Do you reckon I was any help?" he asked, cocking one bushy eyebrow.

"I should just say you were," Stan agreed, while Tubby held out his tobacco pouch, now fat and healthy looking from the ship's stores.

"Well," Ben took a generous pipeful of tobacco in an absent-minded way, "could you manage without a cook for the remainder of the trip? I've left the meal ready, and there's a fine plum duff just right for eatin'."

"You mean—you'd like to leave us?" Stan asked, a twinkle in his eyes.

Ben grinned.

"I ain't never deserted ship before," he said, "but it'll be better all round if I was to vanish."

"Have you any money?"

"I'll manage. I think I can get back to the old Country without too much trouble. I knows my way about."

"Hm!" Stan pondered for a moment, then nodded: "We can't legally let you go, Ben; but if you made your escape—well!"

"Thanks." Ben turned on his heels and went. He was not seen again.

The story of the Pirate Sealer made headline news all over the civilised world, and money poured in to reimburse Sigurd Gundorf for the loss of his ship. His catch, and the sealskins of a dozen other ships, were, of course, safe enough in the holds of the *Bear*.

When it was all over, the inquiries ended, the rush of reporters and cameramen finished, Stan and Tubby sailed for England. Stan took with him the few possessions belonging to Jimmy Staton.

It had been impossible to keep Jimmy's name, or the part he had played, out of the evidence. His death, which had resulted in saving Gundorf and his crew from being marooned on the ice, was seized on by the Press and given spectacular headlines. Stan, looking for something with which to comfort Staton's friends and relatives, cut out one headline which he thought epitomised the whole thing. It read:

"Seal pirate reforms—gives life for boyhood friend."

THE END